Love & Hunger

LOVE &
HUNGER

VICKERY TURNER

E. P. DUTTON   NEW YORK

First published in the United States in 1988 by E. P. Dutton,
a division of NAL Penguin Inc.,
2 Park Avenue, New York, N.Y. 10016.

Originally published in Great Britain under the title Lovers of Africa.

Library of Congress Cataloging-in-Publication Data

Turner, Vickery.
Love and hunger.

Originally published as: Lovers of Africa.
London : V. Gollancz, 1987.
I. Title.
PS3570.U748L6   1988   813'.54   87-36504
ISBN: 0-525-24638-X

1 3 5 7 9 10 8 6 4 2

First American Edition

Contents

Part One

Dear Henry,

I hope your life is more interesting than mine right now. Nothing is happening and there is nothing on the horizon. I've been having a lot of dreams and that's about it.

Last night I dreamed that I was on a train going to Moscow with Mr Dartey. It was an interminable journey and must have taken the entire night to dream up all those long waits at stations and slow chugging across snow-covered plains. I think that it represented the interminably boring work I do for Mr Dartey and was my subconscious protest.

The dream was neither brightly coloured nor monochrome, more a gentle assortment of slate greys and grey blues, and some deep blues, rather like the colours in Renoir's *Les Parapluies*. At intervals I would jump off the train in my deep blue velvet coat and grey sable hat amid a swirl of grey smoke and buy a chicken sandwich for Mr Dartey or a bottle of wine; and the train, which at all other times was ponderous and slow, would suddenly leave the station at considerable speed, while I was still waiting for my change. Then I would run after the train, holding up my heavy skirt and petticoats and Mrs Dartey, his mother, would lean out of the window with an evil triumphant smile. I would always manage to grab the end of the train, tearing my blue velvet jacket, almost losing my grey sable hat, but pulling myself aboard.

It would have been more appropriate to dream something

with an African theme, since everything about Mr Dartey is unrelentingly African. Perhaps something with Freudian undertones: the extinct Mount Kenya spewing out red hot lava for fifty miles around, the sort of thing most impressionable young women who work for him might dream about. Mr Dartey is a touch volcanic, a sort of mute pressure cooker bubbling away inexplicably. But the daily work is definitely not volcanic and a long, boring train ride with his mother looking out of the window just about sums it all up.

Mr Dartey writes long dry papers on famines and international aid which I type up for him. These are sent out to be printed and I'm not sure where they go after that. Governments and universities I suppose. I'm sure if any president or prime minister wanted to understand their contents he would first get some poor underling to break it down for ordinary human comprehension. I pride myself, having now worked for Mr Dartey for three weeks, on being able to get the gist of these reports, some of it anyway.

I've never had a conversation with Mr Dartey, he mostly hands me things with a grunt, but I have a feeling that he is probably as incomprehensible as his reports. Mrs Dartey senior interviewed me for the job and told me what to do. There doesn't seem to be a Mr Dartey senior or a Mrs Dartey junior, but who knows, he may have six wives and dozens of children living out in Northern Kenya or Somalia.

The biographical notes on the inside cover of one of his books say that he works for DAF (Development and Food for the Third World) and has devoted his life to famine relief and agricultural development in Africa and can speak six tribal languages. I'm not sure he can speak English though because he's only ever grunted to me. (Admittedly he can write a sort of unreadable English). His mother came into his study the other day and talked to him at great length and he answered her in low monosyllables. She was trying to persuade him to come to a dinner party on Friday evening and apparently, from what she was saying, he must have indicated that he didn't have time because he was going back to Africa soon and he wanted to get all his work done.

I realized that this meant it will be a short term job. That's all right by me. I would prefer something a little less concentrated. There is an atmosphere of furious energy around Mr Dartey which on the whole I find very admirable. But it's his, not mine. All that steam-powered, hyperactive zeal pulsating in the next room is quite enervating to my own manic energy, and I become a subdued, deferential typist the minute I arrive in the morning.

Sometimes when his study door is left ajar, I can see him sitting at his desk, his dark eyebrows contorted in concentration and an angry look on his face. He picks his nose and stares at the wall. It is fortunate that Mr Dartey picks his nose and coughs in an obnoxious way, sort of spews up into his hand and wipes it down his trousers. It is most fortunate because Mr Dartey is most beautiful to look at and it has taken some odious habits like these to stop my heart from fluttering every time I look at him. I'm sure he has set many a heart a-flutter: he looks like a particularly exceptional advertising model, the sort one sees standing manfully on yachts or driving a Mercedes Benz beside a beautiful woman in glossy magazines. He has dark, almost blackish hair, turquoise blue eyes and very tanned skin. He's about six foot three and very broad. I'm sure if he gets tired of famine relief, he could make a fortune working as a model, if he would just stop picking his nose.

He picks his nose when he is talking to his mother who is the most refined and fastidious of women. She floats around in delicate pink and mauve chiffon on her romantic days and tailored black suits with white blouses on her crisp and formal days. It is her house I'm working in, and it is just like her, decorated in flimsy pastel shades and fabrics, with a few dark areas like Mr Dartey's study.

Her groceries, even potatoes, are all delivered from Harrods and so are bouquets of flowers; currently it's baby roses and anemones in little vases all over the place. In a bored moment the other day I counted how many roses I could see and there were six dozen. I thought that was far too many for one house and I took some home with me.

In the bathroom there are monogrammed hand towels with satin edges and scented soap in the shape of flowers, which are removed quickly after they have been used once. I would love

11

to know where the discarded soap goes, in a dustbin at the back I suppose. If I could find it I would sell it on a stall in the Portobello Road. Anything unsightly is offensive to Mrs Dartey; I can see the pain in her eyes and slight twitch of the cheek, when she catches me eating a doughnut during my coffee break. Yet she will engage in a long conversation with her son while he picks his nose, staring right past the noxious activity and into his eyes as though he were playing a Mozart violin concerto, exquisitely. And Mr Dartey looks vacantly at his mother and continues undisturbed by any reproach.

I see all this from my vantage point in the corner behind the typewriter in what is virtually a hallway. Neither Mr Dartey nor his mother are struck by any great chords of liberalism and see no indignity in the fact that I am stuck out in the hallway like a coatstand. They are both very patrician. I think that is one of the reasons he merely grunts at me, which must be a standard way of addressing a humble typist, and she says good morning with a gracious smile and then drifts past. After that I am pretty much left to my own devices. I am permitted to go into the kitchen and make myself tea or coffee and then I have a conversation with the cook. She also treats me as an inferior being and shouts at me when I pick the wrong cup or fill the kettle too full. I've heard her shouting at Mrs Dartey however, so I assume she treats everyone as inferior beings, which makes the social scale in the house a little more interesting. The cook's name is Gabrielle and she came to England from Germany thirty-four years ago, though one might think she had arrived yesterday as her accent is totally innocent of any English inflections.

Today she told me how the British and Americans flattened Dresden; she was born there and most of her family were killed by the bombing. "A beautiful family and a beautiful city," she said in a manner which I identified, in my usual paranoid way, as accusatory. I was not quite sure what to say. Sorry hardly seemed appropriate nor did some homily about the horror of war, but I didn't have to say anything. She said, "The British and the West Germans are in the Common Market now and we all have the same enemy."

She paused until I said, "Who's that?"

"Materialism. Materialism and godlessness. It will destroy us all."

I did not feel that this applied to me as Mr Dartey subscribes to the theory that workers should be poorly paid and thus I am not in a position to be materialistic. I should think this means that I am saved from a certain amount of godlessness too. I put up with this poor pay because the job is reasonably flexible and I can take time off for auditions and interviews. In this case the fact that Mr Dartey can only grunt works to my advantage.

I knock on his study door and he says "Eh!"

Then I go in and ask for a couple of hours off and he says "Uh" which I always interpret as "Yes, certainly." So I say "Thank you very much" and leave quickly.

On Wednesday I had an interview at the BBC Television Centre. It was for the part of a student. "No make up, and they'll never guess you're over the hill," my agent said. Did I tell you I have a new agent? His name is Jeffrey Bird and he has an office in Camden Town over a bakery, so his office always smells of hot bread. I lied to him about my age and took a couple of years off as I think I'm too old to have achieved so little. So don't forget I'm now twenty-six. Engrave it somewhere. When I'm successful I will tell the truth. Successful people can do anything.

Love,
Lili

It was the third time that Henry had read his sister's letter. She had not written for several months; now came this sign that her situation was a little healthier. She had made a brief call to the family to say that she was going to work for a Mr Dartey and they had been speculating ever since as to what sort of work it was.

The fact that she had phoned was in itself remarkable. She had virtually given up phoning so as to avoid lectures on, advice about, and remedies for her wasted life. She kept in communication with them by writing to Henry. In the past when things were not quite so bad Lili had written to Henry regularly and in detail. They had agreed that when she was famous, he would use these letters as the basis for a biography of Lili Smith. So far things were not quite working according to plan. Recognition on the lowest level, a modicum of achievement and self-respect, let alone fame and success, seemed highly elusive.

Henry folded the letter carefully and tucked it into his pocket. He was sitting on the Intercity express from Leeds to London, having spent the weekend competing in an archery tournament on the Yorkshire Moors. He had wished that he had brought something else to read, and stared out of the window at fields and cows flashing by. It was like watching a rewind of a pastoral videotape. He glanced down at the crumpled copy of the *Daily Express* lying on the seat between him and his fellow passenger. It was open at the William Hickey column, which included a photograph of a dark-haired man in evening dress; underneath the photograph Henry recognized the name Dartey.

"Excuse me," said Henry to the man next to him. "Have you finished with this?"

"Oh yes," said the man, who had been looking at Henry's legs which seemed like pipe cleaners inside his trousers extending down from a powerful torso. The incongruous body sat on the seat rather like a ventriloquist's dummy. The man had not seen Henry sit down and wondered how he arrived in this position.

Henry took the paper in his large hands; they were over-developed hands with gnarled fingers. Each finger, the man noticed, had an independent strength so that although it was large and strong, it had the lightness of a dancer. Yes that was it: it was as if each of his fingers danced to its own tune. Most fingers on ordinary hands generally follow the pattern of the other fingers, but not Henry's. As he tore out the William Hickey column with great deftness, only the fingers actually engaged in the occupation descended to do their work, the others remained poised in the air at odd angles as though doing pliés or arabesques.

14

The photograph from the paper had a caption underneath it saying that Edmund Dartey was in London after several years in Africa. His mother, the Honourable Mrs Dartey, had given a dinner party for him. Henry folded the piece of newspaper and tucked it into his pocket alongside Lili's letter.

When the train drew into King's Cross and the passengers began shuffling around and lifting down suitcases, Henry suddenly dropped to the floor and slithered along the compartment with a quick decisive motion. He moved like a lizard dragging a useless tail of pipecleaner legs behind him, and disappeared through the door into the guard's van. He reappeared in a wheelchair after the train stopped, propelling himself with great rapidity along the platform to the ticket barrier. There was a minor scuffle as his wheelchair would not go through the barrier and he was sent round another way. Then he raced to the taxi queue. A taxi driver who was planning to get out of his cab to help, found that Henry was already inside the cab pulling his folded wheelchair in after him, well before the driver could be of any assistance.

Edmund Dartey walked slowly down the stairs holding a cup of coffee. He felt submerged. He had felt submerged ever since he had arrived in England and come to stay in this house. After Africa, everything here seemed enclosing and submerging. The walls felt closer, and his mother, who had been a sort of distant spiritual symbol for the last fifteen years, seemed to be everywhere. He passed the kitchen where he could see his mother and Gabrielle bending towards each other muttering in their customary belligerent fashion. He moved on quickly, not wishing to be observed, and went into the study.

The study was quiet and dark; it reminded him of his father. It was the only place in the house that was sombre and masculine, with a heavy burnished mahogany desk and dark oak bookcases lining the walls. It was the only place in the house that evidenced learning and literature. The rest of the house was an ode to femininity, devoid of books, with flimsy silk curtains and fragile antique furniture, chairs with the slenderest of legs that made him cautious about sitting down, and carpets of the palest oatmeal and fuchsia that dared him to walk across them in his heavy boots.

He had dim memories of his father sitting at the desk in the study. He had died thirty-two years ago, two years after Gabrielle had arrived; but he could still feel his father's spirit in the room, a sort of kindly removed forbearance. He liked to imagine he could still smell his father there. He could remember his smell. As a child he was, like all other children, very aware of a person's smell, something that was quite close to their spiritual essence. His father did not smell, like most fathers, of tobacco and sweat. His father smelled of damp earth and clay, old books and hot tea, all mingled in a kindly, subtle way.

Through the window he could see the typing girl coming up the path to the house. Her hair, which had been very fluffy and pink, like candy floss, the first day, was by degrees becoming a sensible reddish-blonde. And he noticed that her thin arms had grown slightly plumper over the last three weeks.

She seemed a strange, impenetrable female, rather out of touch with the art of being a typist. He would probably have to get rid of her and hire someone more efficient. He had noticed that if she did not understand his handwriting, she would not come to him and ask him to interpret but would type something she considered appropriate. Some of it was quite creative.

She stared at him a great deal with cold analytical eyes, but she looked away quickly if he returned her stare. They rarely, if ever, looked at each other at the same time. It would be sensible to dismiss her immediately. He would get far more done if it was not for the fact that he had to keep a firm eye on the typed copies and correct that damn girl's work.

The girl rang the front door bell and Catherine Dartey went to answer. He could hear her passing the study door and crossing the hall. She had told several people at last night's dinner that her son was planning to stay in England permanently. Perhaps she was under the impression that if she made enough people believe something then it would really happen. Whatever she thought, he had in fact come for a brief visit, enough time to talk to his publisher write some articles, be a dutiful son and then go. It was difficult to live in her house. It was a step back in time. On the surface the mother-son relationship may have seemed to change over the years, but underneath it was cemented in concrete. There was still that unspoken expectancy that he should be dutiful and obedient and see the world through her eyes, and that any departure from that was an insult to her authority. It was strange. He had hardly given his mother a thought for fifteen years and now he was having to think of her every day.

He heard the front door open, and a blast of air from outside pushed the study door ajar: now he could see the girl standing there while his mother examined her.

"What a pretty dress," said Catherine.

The girl looked down at her dress as if to discover what she had put on that morning. It was a black dress with short sleeves, and a skirt that seemed too long for a typist's skirt. She had worn it every day for the last two weeks; even he had noticed that.

The girl gave a faint smile and said, "Thank you." She moved past Catherine and went immediately to her desk in the hall. She put a shopping bag on the floor beside the desk. He wondered what she had in it. What did typists usually keep in bags? Women's magazines and knitting he supposed. And of course her doughnut. She always ate a doughnut with her coffee. He noticed that the deep hollows in her cheeks were filling out. He wondered what else she ate besides doughnuts. She ate her doughnut in the same way that people who have starved for a long time eat their food, not with delight at the taste or the sensation of eating, but with great solemnity signifying that eating was a serious business.

His mother watched the girl and stood hovering for a few seconds; then she went slowly upstairs. He knew there was nothing for her to do up there. After the elaborate procedure of dressing, there was little else for her to do.

The girl came into the study and picked up his papers from the tray. She had to type up everything he put in that tray. It occurred to him to say something about her creative interpretation of some of his sentences.

"Er . . ."

The girl stared at him in a fixed and amazed way, as though noticing a runner bean starting to grow slowly out of his head.

He changed his mind. Perhaps he should just fire her and get it over with. He would do that tomorrow. He nodded at her in a dismissive way and she turned and went out.

Dear Henry,

I have moved! I was in debt with my rent and was seriously considering finding a bench on Victoria Station. Fortunately I met this rather strange actor called Charles Spedding—he reminds me of a white rabbit; he is very pale and his eyelashes and eyebrows are scarcely visible.

He goes away a lot and needs somebody to feed his cats and water his plants. His wife used to do it but she's moved out after eighteen years of marriage and taken the children. So for providing my feeding and watering services I am allowed to live rent free.

His house is at Notting Hill Gate just round the corner from where I lived before. It's a typical married actor's house, full of stripped pine furniture, polished wooden floors, rocking horses and plants.

Charlie is hard work when he's around and I certainly earn my free lodgings. He has several glasses of Scotch and wine every evening and then makes a pass, a sort of lunging pass trying to get handfuls of breast and buttocks like a neophyte rapist. After I've pushed him back in his armchair he bemoans his fate as an actor. Recently he's been in several plays with television personalities as stars that have toured endlessly around Britain "like a plane with no landing gear" and never made it to the West End. Last Christmas he played Marley's Ghost in Guildford, a part he played twenty years ago in Tunbridge Wells. He is convinced this is a sign of stagnation, that he is an assembly line actor, artistically dead, unstretched, unsung and as miserable as sin. Nightly he contemplates doing something else, perhaps using his degree in chemistry; he toys with that idea for a while, then concludes that he is too old at

18

forty-five, and the chemistry he knows bears no relation to the chemistry of today. He agonizes because he has never used his education, and his acting career, though shallow and not tapping his resources, has exhausted him.

"Spending your life acting is like having a really stupid nymphomaniac girlfriend. You spend your life fucking and then one day you wake up and say what have I done with my life?"

And so he goes on and on. I really can't sympathize with someone who works as much as he does. I would give my ears to be touring endlessly around Britain.

On Saturday I helped him make a Dundee cake and we almost ended up stabbing each other with kitchen knives. Charlie follows recipes as if they are vital chemical formulas. Every grain of sugar, speck of flour and raisin was weighed and measured. This process was tedious beyond belief to me and to prevent myself from screaming I threw things into the bowl when he was peering at the scales. This would make Charlie hysterical. By the time the cake was in the oven we were very close to ending up in pools of blood on the kitchen floor.

Fortunately he'll be going off to Swansea on Friday. He's moaning about that too. He says the landladies in Swansea serve orange squash in juice glasses for breakfast.

So now I have two extremely tedious employers. Of the two, Charlie is a little easier to manage than Mr Dartey, who is remote and stiff.

Sometimes I sit at my desk in the hallway, which receives cold draughts of wind from an outside door, and plan odd things to surprise Mr Dartey. I contemplate running in and doing a can-can or a backward somersault, but I am always held back at the last second by the awful fear that he won't even look up from his desk so that I will be left standing there at the end of it all pretending that I have come in for some paper.

I've tried to imagine how it would be if their roles were reversed and Mr Dartey were an actor with a house in Notting Hill and Charlie were to write papers on famine relief. For a start Charlie would drive me insane with his criticism of my typing; at least Mr Dartey lets everything slide past him, he's just too vague to notice. And if Mr Dartey were an actor he would probably be away starring in films all the time because he is so beautiful—that's if he could learn to open his mouth and say a few words. Then I would have the house to myself all the time. If he came home and made a pass at me like Charlie, I think I would give in just to see what he looked like without a shirt on. He would be a far prettier sight than Charlie who has the alabaster skin of a Victorian lady, invisible hairs on his chest, and a little roll of flesh hanging over his belt. I see all this in its full glory in the morning when he parades around in nothing but a towel. He seems determined to let me see as much of him as possible, whereas Mr Dartey only shows me the top of his head.

I think one of the main reasons I would like to be famous and totally occupied with large scale things is that I would no longer have to worry about the petty foibles of the Charlies and Mr Darteys of this world.

In the meantime I send you the mindless meanderings of a typist who has not heard from her agent in two weeks.

Love,
Lili

P.S. Tell the parents that I have had hundreds of auditions and offers and am trying to decide which one to select.

Dear Lili,

I think it's about time you came home. The parents are nagging me about it assuming that I have some kind of power to bring you home, so please come just to give me a break.

You are a constant topic right now. "Is she eating? She looked so thin the last time she came down." And the long analysis of why you are so thin. Is it from lack of finances or a desire to be extremely thin? I explained to them that you have none of the psychological make up of an anorexic, who on the whole are perfectionists with a desire to please, which could hardly describe you.

They are delighted you have a job even if it is only typing. I have made them promise to keep off their two main themes if you come to visit so you will not hear a whisper of "you're wasting your education" and "you're too old to be drifting."

I cut out a photo of your boss Mr Dartey from the newspaper and will give it to you when you come down. You're right, he is quite pretty but not as pretty as me.

Love,
Henry

P.S. I have a large collection of your letters now. In assembling your biography I'm finding that the suffering, struggling years are stretching out further than is usual in a star's biography. I have decided that I will have to condense these chapters otherwise it might put the reader off.

If you could just bring something out of the bag this year, then it will really help the next few chapters.

Dear Henry,

I will come to visit if you will guarantee that the parents will keep their bargain. With this proviso I think I could come on Saturday morning. But *do* keep them at bay. I don't want a constant harping on my failure as a human being, an ageing human being.

Things are hotting up at work. Today Mr Dartey spoke to me! He didn't look me in the eye as he spoke but they were definitely words. I went into his study to pick up some notes. On his desk were some photographs of children and mothers at a famine relief post in Eritrea. Their bodies were hardly there at all, and in their eyes was the expression of people who have suffered so much that—well, they were almost half way to being free, as if mortal life could no longer dominate them.

I've been typing up things for weeks about these people, but the sight of them shocked me; before I knew it I was saying something to Mr Dartey. Of course it was something totally inappropriate. I said, "Poor creatures, I know what it's like to starve. I ran out of money recently and I had hardly any food for six weeks."

Mr Dartey did not look up. His pen paused for a moment over his note pad and he said, "Starving in London at this point in time is simply an indulgence."

I went back to my desk and made a lot of typing errors.

So Mr Dartey spoke! And proved what I had already thought, that he is a self righteous twit. It's not my fault that most of the world is starving. I think I will look for another job.

See you on Saturday.

Love,
Lili

It was a request Dartey had been dreading. DAF U.K. had asked him to stay in London for another twelve months. As an incentive he had been offered a flat in Little Venice which had just been vacated by another DAF worker. Dartey was anxious to get out of London and was not at all sure that anything could persuade him to stay. But if he did, the flat would be a necessity; it was essential to get out of his mother's house. It was reasonable to return to the nursery for a brief visit but not any longer. He had to get out of the nursery.

He also had to get rid of the typing girl and find someone more effective. Admittedly his handwriting went astray at times but it was not totally illegible and should at least be quite clear to someone who had spent several weeks reading it. The trouble with that girl was that she did not attempt to read it properly. When in doubt she made it up. She would have to go. He would dismiss her this morning and phone the agency for a replacement.

Gabrielle padded in silently bringing him another cup of coffee. He noticed that the girl was swigging her coffee gratefully, holding it in her hands like a small child. Her face looked wasted as though she had been up all night. She still had on her black dress.

22

As though Gabrielle had read his thoughts she walked over to the girl's desk and said, "You've got that black dress on again."

The girl smiled, "Yes, isn't it lovely."

Gabrielle stared at her dress dubiously. "Do you take it off at night?"

The girl looked down at the dress as though expecting the dress to answer; hearing no response she took another swig of coffee and said in confidential tones, "I thought it suitable for this type of work. I didn't want to wear lurex or jeans."

"It's good for a funeral," said Gabrielle and went back to the kitchen where Catherine Dartey was having an argument with the milkman. Gabrielle took the side of the milkman.

Dartey watched the girl stand up and come towards his study. This would be a good opportunity to dismiss her. She knocked on the open door and walked straight in without waiting for him to answer.

She stood there looking at him for a few seconds. She was reasonably pretty in a stark unusual sort of way, though not the sort of girl to turn heads. The sun came through the window and lit a halo around her voluminous hair, transforming her into a recalcitrant fairy on a Christmas tree.

Dartey framed a silent sentence that would be dismissive yet kindly, firm yet not harsh. He coughed and cleared his throat in preparation. But the girl spoke first.

"Would you mind if I have a couple of hours off this morning. I have an interview."

"Er . . ."

"Thank you very much." She leaned forward slightly over the desk and picked up the papers in his tray.

Dartey, thinking to deprive her of employment, put his hand out to take the papers back, and for an instant, a mere second, he held his hand firmly over hers.

It was an extraordinary moment. He had not expected the touch of her skin against his to produce such a sensation. He stared at her in shock, almost accusingly. She too seemed to be experiencing something because she shivered involuntarily and then withdrew her hands, leaving him holding the papers. She lowered her eyes quickly and went out of the room.

After that he slowly picked up his pen and wrote, "In examining President Nyerere's current concession to the World Bank, with the devaluation of the shilling and increased producer prices, we have to ask . . ." It took an hour to write that. At the end of the hour he completed the sentence. ". . . we have to ask if his socialist goals have been compromised."

There was silence from her desk. He knew why. She had nothing to type. All her work was on his desk.

About the time he was completing his first sentence, she left for her interview. He watched her through the window with an acute interest.

On Saturday Henry caught the train up to London to see Lili at her request. She simply did not feel strong enough to go home and face the family's reproaches.

Henry came speeding down the road towards her house having caught a bus from Victoria to Notting Hill Gate. To get on the bus he threw himself forward on to the platform then twisted around, folded his wheelchair, and pulled it after him. The stairs at the station had also been negotiated quite efficiently. He had parked his wheelchair at the top of the stairs and said to a suitably strong pair of bodies, "I say, could you give me a lift?" Which they did.

Lili stood on her front doorstep and observed Henry flying down the street towards her, like a large doll in a runaway pushchair. She had not seen him for several weeks and was stunned by the extravagant beauty of her brother, extravagant being the operative word: everything about his head and face was a little too much. There was rather too much curly hair of an almost translucent shiny blonde; the head was a little too large to balance the tapering insignificant body; the eyes were a little too blue and too large. There was also a steady perceptive quality to the eyes which was a little too much; it bordered on the hypnotic.

"You're absolutely right Henry. You are prettier than Mr Dartey," said Lili guiding him up the front path to the house.

She took him on a tour of all the rooms and then led him

into the tiny brick-walled garden where they sat under a laburnum tree and watched Charlie's cats playing in the tangled wilderness which constituted the garden. A large rusty refrigerator sat in a corner in an imbroglio of dandelions and stinging nettles, and a dozen different waist-high weeds and grasses filled a space which was once a lawn. A cracked concrete path led past drains and dustbins up to the French windows. The laburnum tree stood alone in its single beauty, casting a blessing of suffused light through its leaves on to the mess beneath it and giving it a certain grace.

"I can't go home, not just yet," said Lili.

Henry nodded understandingly like an old man. He was twenty-two years old, yet he had a mature sort of wisdom, almost a craftiness.

"I went for an audition yesterday and they asked me to come again on Monday."

"What's it for?"

"A play. In a pub in Clapham. I'd get very little money."

Henry picked up a kitten and tried to keep it still in his lap. "It may be *the* part."

"Yes."

"You know you're writing a lot about this Dartey guy. From an historical perspective, do you want to have so much about him included in the story of your life?"

"I just write about him because he's there. That's what my life is at the moment, sitting in the hallway outside his study."

"O.K. I'll just call it your Dartey period."

"I haven't brought you up to date with Mr Dartey."

"Oh?"

"Well it was quite an extraordinary thing really. I picked up some papers from his desk and he went to grab them away from me. I don't know why. He had something he wanted to say I think. Anyway our hands touched."

"And?"

"That was it. Then I went out."

"So?"

"It made me shiver. There was a definite physical thing that happened when our hands touched."

"Sounds like sex to me."

25

"Yes . . . but two bodies can't just touch . . . Some thought process has to go on first. I was wondering what it came out of. From me perhaps it's a hostility, an intense resentment about the work, and from him its . . . well maybe he's getting angry about my typing. And you know actually I'm getting better."

"Obviously not good enough. All bosses want to bounce on bad typists."

"Oh."

"I mean, if the typing isn't good what else does he have to think about?"

Lili sighed. "Do you think I'm going to be a pathetic dilettante for the rest of my life, struggling to support myself, working for awful bosses like Mr Dartey?"

"No I don't think they'll all be like Mr Dartey."

"You are a bastard Henry."

Later on, for one fraction for a second, Lili saw Henry as others might see him. He was struggling face downwards on the platform of the bus, twisting around clumsily to reach out for his wheelchair and Lili saw him as a pathetic cripple with little hope for his future. His brief moment of independence dissolved as the bus conductor and passengers lifted him into a seat and he watched passively as they folded his wheelchair.

Lili and Henry had an unspoken pact to see each other as super heroes, and she quickly returned to this concept with mental ferocity, for it needed great ferocity.

The outward signs for Henry were not good. He could not walk, he had a university degree but no particular skills, and finding employment was, as Henry put it, "becoming a way of life." His employment was finding employment.

Lili in her turn might have been considered pathetic by any rational person. Nearing her twenty-ninth birtuday, an age when there should have been some sign that she was on the right track, she merely had a series of insignificant bouts in the theatre behind her, none of which had revealed any particular talent or lack of it. Yet she still clutched this passionate desire to her bosom, this need to be an actress. Her family considered her misguided. All of them that is except Henry. In his eyes she was a woman of infinite possibilities.

The letters were a way of confirming this: Henry had

convinced her that one day he would produce these letters in a book which would provide a detailed study of an ascending star. On a good day Lili could see this as a definite reality but mostly she wrote the letters to help Henry, to fill out his day, and bring him a piece of her world. Currently, however, their worlds were similar, filled with rejection and a bleak sense of uselessness. But she knew that these letters from her provided him with activity. He would edit them, type them out, then file them away. Often he would discuss "point of view". Would he write from the standpoint of her distinguished career comparing it with her past struggle, as an interesting counterpoint, or would it be purely chronological? They would discuss this at length and come to no particular conclusion. The letters, like their search for employment, had become a goal in themselves. The last thing he had said while being lifted into his seat on the bus was, "Keep writing the letters."

After the "incident" between them Dartey looked for a sign in the girl to see if it had any effect on her. The only change was in her work. She made a greater effort to understand his handwriting and there were fewer mistakes in her typing. Other than that, she remained as impersonal as ever, enclosed in her own world, oblivious to him.

There were still a few occasions when he caught her staring at him, but she quickly looked away. She stared at him as one might stare at a vacuum cleaner in a shop window. There was no invitation in it.

Even so, it was hard for him not to feel her presence. When the door was closed he still felt distracted by her, as if he were close enough to feel her breath on his face. When the door was open he watched her head bending over her desk and observed the texture of the skin on her cheeks: sometimes it was pale and powdery, other times glossy and pink. She wore strange colours around her eyes, plum and purple, sometimes apple green, sometimes no colour at all; then with her pale eyelashes, light freckles and her face washed clean of paint, she became a child. But this was a child with wise eyes, whose maturity could be painted on with bright, broad strokes or it could descend overnight if she went without sleep and she would come to work, drawn, soggy, and years older.

She began to wear other clothes besides the black dress but they were similar long, drab garments that she wore with boots and black stockings. It gave her a sort of workhouse appearance and added to her prohibitive stance. He could not speak to her or make any overtures because her manner clearly indicated that she was here to work and work alone.

Inexplicably he had given in to the pressure from DAF and agreed to stay in London. After he moved to his new flat near the canal in Little Venice, the girl continued to work for him, but only in the mornings as she had acquired an acting job that she worked on in the afternoons and evenings. This made her even more remote and preoccupied.

She made no comment on the fact that the flat was almost entirely without furniture. The previous owner had omitted to remove a couch, or perhaps the removal men had refused to touch it as it was extremely ugly, being covered in shiny orange plastic. Other than that he had purchased two desks and two chairs for his work, a mattress to sleep on, and two cups, a kettle, and a spoon for the kitchen. The flat was dominated by the shiny orange couch which caught the sunlight during the day and the electric light at night and shone like a massive traffic beacon.

He had for some time been engaged in a correspondence with the British African League about a series of Saturday morning lectures at the Linwood Comprehensive School in Battersea. He had been asked to give six lectures, the first being on socialism and capitalism in East Africa. The girl handled the correspondence and for some unknown reason it aroused her interest. Perhaps it was the possible theatricality of it, an event that would require a performance from him, rather than the mere writing of words. Whatever it was, she opened up the handbills and posters when they arrived with something akin to delight, studying the design and the colour, and even hanging one on the bare walls of the living room.

Finally one day she came into his room (he no longer had a study, just a stark white room, empty except for the desk and chair) and asked, "Do you want me to type the notes for the lecture."

"I don't have any notes."

"Oh." She looked at him curiously.

He observed her childlike soft face which would have been innocent, almost vacuous, were it not for those cool, analytical eyes. The eyes seemed to miss nothing.

She smiled at him. Not a warm, come hither smile, but a polite one, a totally asexual, polite smile, suitable for a typist to her employer. And then she went back to her desk.

She left him to think about his lecture, his lack of notes (he wondered now if he should make some, he had always been able to wing it before) and about her—why did he think about her? He probably thought about her because she was there. He was making no effort to find female companionship, because it was that, an effort. Women seemed to be needy creatures, at least the women he attracted all needed a certain amount of emotional propping up. He was a listener, and he had discovered that anyone who was a listener was a mobile psychiatric couch. He had spent a good deal of his life listening to and retreating from talkative women. He was a listener by default. He was not without enthusiasm for expressing his own opinions but he was not insistent and somehow he was usually pipped at the post. Then his own conversation had to be confined to advice and consolation.

He did not feel like rushing out right now and getting involved on a grand scale, having to pay for a sexual engagement by listening for hours to tales about ex-husbands and old boyfriends or fathers. Perhaps that was why he was indulging himself in the fantasy over the girl. It was safe. He was the boss. He could replace her at any given moment.

The girl was right. Where were the notes for his lecture? He sat down and gave some thought to postwar industrialization in East Africa and foreign capital in the post-colonial economy. What was the point of giving a lecture? He avoided thinking about this question because it generated a larger one. What was the point of his last fifteen years in Africa? He was trying to avoid that question because he had no answer for it.

He spent a couple of hours juggling with the theory that

underdevelopment was the product of capitalist penetration and contrasting it with the orthodox development theory, the one he had subscribed to when he first arrived in Africa. He had assumed then that all countries worked through various stages of underdevelopment until they had become fully fledged clones of France or Great Britain. He had once assumed all sorts of things. He had once seen himself as a saintly worker coming to till the soil and bring food to hungry bellies; now he saw himself as caught in a mesh, one cog in a wheel that created more hungry bellies than it saved.

He stared at the shiny orange sofa and imagined the girl lying on it with one hand stretched out beseechingly towards him. He felt beset by a mental paralysis that prevented him from getting rid of either the girl or the sofa. He would wait for circumstances to remove them.

Dear Henry,

There's only one thing worse than being an unemployed actor and that's being an employed one. We're rehearsing in the theatre which was formerly a storage room at the back of *The Princess Louise* and smells of stale beer and puke, which is the least of my troubles. The real problem is the play and the director which is just about everything. The play was written by Eleanor Bright, a housewife from Birmingham. It's her first play and she knows nothing about the theatre; and now all she knows about is rooms at the back of pubs and a group of people in total disarray.

At our first reading the director told us that the play, owing to the writer's lack of craft, had no beginning, middle and ending, a simple requirement of any play, but merely an extended beginning. Therefore it was incumbent upon him as a director and us, if we had any ideas, to come up with some improvements. Well, of course, everyone has a thousand different ideas and the poor woman who wrote it sits there and looks totally bewildered. She said that the last time she came to London was for the Festival of Britain in 1952 when she was a small girl and it was marginally more amusing then, even though she got lost on the underground and her brother was sick in Lyon's Corner House.

The plot of her play is based on an experience of her mother. It's quite dramatic really, but the problem is that Eleanor has written a lot of scenes that are not relevant and left out scenes that should be there. The story is floating around somewhere in another dimension and even if it were to assemble itself quite tidily it would still be a simple melodrama.

One wonders why so many good plays get ignored and bad plays get done. It must be because a good critical faculty is as rare as fairy dust and works are chosen by exhausted and confused producers who know they must choose something eventually.

I have discovered to my amazement that I have the leading role, which under any other circumstances would be quite a coup. Everything here is either discordant or pathetic, so really things haven't changed in my life one little bit. It was very easy to get this part. I only saw the director a couple of times and "Pow!" that was it. I feel like somebody who has found a thousand pounds and then discovers they are all counterfeit.

Anyway I'm going to do my best. The director, whose name is Ian Harding, is extremely serious, and when he's not seeing this play in terms of the fall of capitalism and the collapse of the world's monetary system, he sees it in terms of nakedness. He has always wanted to see a naked dance on stage as a symbol of the helplessness of man in today's society. Well if he thinks I'm going to dance naked in a small room at the back of a pub, he's got another think coming.

He has to be watched! Every day he says a little more about creativity being a process of stripping and showing the real man that we have concealed since childhood. He devotes at least an hour every day to a monologue on uncovering the creative soul, but this monologue itself when stripped to its essence just comes down to taking your knickers off in public. I've told him I'll take my clothes off if he'll take his off. And you should see him! He's not unlike Charlie with the same white, foam-rubber body, except that he is darker with glasses and a pointed beard.

I'm still not quite sure why I was given this part. Even the most meagre role has been so completely elusive for so long and then all of a sudden a part simply falls into my lap. Admittedly, it's not in the most salubrious of theatres, but it's a job. As the old saying goes, "If your name's written on it . . ."

I'm still working for Mr Dartey in the mornings. Ian Harding does not like to start rehearsing till after lunch, so I have two jobs and am working from nine in the morning till ten at night every day. I need the money though I must say, even with two jobs I'm probably only earning as much as a girl in Woolworths. Right now I'm on the tube going from Warwick Avenue to Clapham.

Mr Dartey has started to give a series of lectures on Saturday mornings in Battersea, not all that far from my pub. I felt obliged to attend at least one of them, as his flat has been littered with posters and handbills advertising the great event.

I think he was quite surprised to see me in the audience. I slipped in late and took some notes, on the assumption that his speech would have to be more coherent than those erudite books and articles of his, and I might learn something. He stopped talking for a few seconds after he saw me and stared as if he'd seen a ghost. It seemed an interminable time to me and I was beginning to think I should leave. I had no idea why my presence should cause such a disturbance, after all he sees me every day. I suppose seeing me in another context might have been strange, though not particularly earth shattering.

Anyway he gathered his wits about him and gave quite an interesting lecture. I think he's one of those upper middle class fellows who is trying to absolve himself of guilt by espousing the cause of the downtrodden African. He quoted the writings of Oginda Odinga who was a Kenyan nationalist leader in the forties and fifties. He said the British Labour Government encouraged co-operative societies after the Second World War but hemmed them around with restrictions and trade regulation which were supposed to help Africans but instead worked against them and left the field open to Asians and white traders. Africans could not raise loans from banks because of their communal land ownership; banks would only accept an individual land title as security on a loan. He said that the confidence and ability of the African was undermined in a multitude of different ways.

Mr Dartey's constant theme seems to be the lack of consideration given to the African way of doing things and that the problems in post-colonial societies cannot be compared with anything in our own history where we had an ascendant native bourgeoisie as opposed to a foreign imperialistic bourgeoisie.

He is comparing socialist economies in East Africa with capitalist economies and seeing if any comparisions can be drawn as to which is better suited for the African. As far as I could gather, because of their colonial history anything is pretty disastrous right now.

Mr Dartey seemed to be making a better argument for socialism and stated that the revolution in Ethiopia could be an example of what is to come in the rest of Africa, which has now reached the place where Ethiopia was ten years ago. He said that the peasant in Zaire has nothing in common with President Mobutu, who is the tenth richest man in the world, and that Africa is engaged in a class struggle. He finished by saying that the socialization of Africa would result in a profound crisis in Europe which is kept afloat by Africa. He announced this with some satisfaction, like a vengeful priest doling out punishment for sins.

During the question and answer period, several people leaped up and challenged Mr Dartey's somewhat revolutionary approach. He skated around that by saying he was examining revolution as a possibility and not actually espousing it.

The questioners were all African and not one of them liked the idea of socialism. The white people in the audience obviously did not feel qualified to speak. One tall handsome man who had the chiselled features of a North African said that he had recently visited Ethiopia and that the average Ethiopian had no idea what the revolution was about. In Addis Ababa, across from the United Nations Economic Commission for Africa, stands a thirty foot high statue of Lenin, a white man who meant nothing to most Ethiopians. He went into a shop in a southern town where a large picture of Andropov was hanging on the wall and he asked the shopkeeper who it was:

the shopkeeper said he didn't know. This brought giggles from the audience.

The chairman, an incredibly voluptuous blonde lady in a velvet cloak, brought the meeting to a close before Mr Dartey could state his case any further. He was surrounded by people asking more questions and the lady chairman latched on to him and guided him out of the hall. She was obviously pleased with the response to the lecture and delighted with Mr Dartey. I don't think she had met him before and seemed quite gleeful upon discovering that he is *so* beautiful. He must have an extremely active sex life because every woman he meets must just drool and throw her clothes off.

Which reminds me. I must rush off to rehearsal now and hope that our dear director does not return to his usual theme of nakedness. It has been my experience that inside every "serious" director there is a crass ringmaster who justifies every bit of splashy theatrics as an emanation of his creative soul but on a subterranean level realises that it will *sell tickets*.

Love
Lili

The last play Dartey had seen was *I Will Marry When I Want* by Ngugi and Ngugi at the Kamiriithu Cultural Centre at Limuru. He had been dragged along by the Dutch Red Cross nurse who slept with him whenever he was in that area. That play's passion had been far more than anything he experienced with the nurse, and he wondered at the time who received the benefit of that passion. The authors of the play were, like most African authors, angry. They made the expected thrusts against British imperialists and missionaries who held the Bible in their left hand and a gun in their right, and made Africans "beggars in our own land". They complained that today a prosperous African was merely a watchdog ensuring the transference of their hard-earned profits to Europe.

Dartey could not argue with the play's premise, but he wondered about the audience. How could a play be effective if it only preached to the converted? This play must have made one or two leaps beyond this boundary because it was eventually banned and one of the writers put in detention without trial. But still Dartey was not convinced that a play was the best forum for any idea beyond mere entertainment.

Now here he was sitting in London's most obscure theatre having this same mental debate and wondering whether the discomfort of the hard folding seat and the oppressively drab surroundings were a test of the audience's asceticism.

He had come to see the girl in her play. It was a definite statement, there was no escaping that. Tomorrow morning she would look at him over her typewriter and he would be obliged to make some comment like, "Well done", or "Most edifying", or whatever you were supposed to say to actresses after a performance.

He had been disconcerted when she came to the lecture. It was strange to see her in another context. When she had walked into the hall he had felt suddenly exposed, as if somehow she were able to dissect him and uncover his preoccupation with her. She had taken notes. Why did she take notes and what was she planning to do with them?

The following Monday the girl's first words were, "I learned a lot from your lecture. It made me want to go to Africa."

"It wasn't meant to be a travelogue," he had said. She had taken that the wrong way and gone off to do her typing.

Later in the day he had tried to start a conversation by asking her about the play. She had handed him a xeroxed sheet of paper with details of time and place and the cast, and that was the end of that conversation.

As verbal communication didn't seem to be their forte he had chosen another opportunity to watch her, but he had not bargained for this theatre. The Actors South Theatre was a room at the back of *The Princess Louise*, a large, neglected pub on the Wandsworth/Clapham border. He had walked through a poorly lit saloon bar with stained peeling wallpaper and torn linoleum. A group of sad regulars and one aged mongrel sat around as though enduring some kind of penance and watching the theatre-goers troop past them with a dull suspicion.

In the dark, musty back room Dartey observed a collection

of small mushrooms growing near the ceiling above his seat. He had thought he could slip out at the end of the play without the girl noticing but in this cramped room she could not possibly miss him. He had not expected to have such an intimate acquaintance with the production; even sitting in the back row he was less than twelve feet from the stage.

The room filled slowly with an assortment of people of an artistic incline, a grim bunch studying the xeroxed sheet of paper which obviously served as a programme.

A youth in a wheelchair had parked himself at the end of a row and was engaged in a conversation with a woman who told him she had written the play.

"I didn't know anything about plays," the woman was saying, "So my son Jason went to the library and found *Miss Julie* by August Strindberg. Well at first we thought August was a woman . . . Anyway everyone was going on at me about structure. Structure, you must have structure. So I studied Strindberg to see if a bit of structure would rub off on me."

"And did it?" the youth in the wheelchair asked. He was staring at Dartey with an undisguised interest and when he caught his eye he smiled and nodded as though they were old friends.

"Oh, good grief no. I mean where do I stand in relation to Strindberg? The introduction said that he represented the plight of modern man but that he wasn't as great as Kierkegaard and Nietzsche. So Jason went to the library again and got the books on them."

'And did that help?'' The youth was continuing to glance at Dartey from time to time.

"Well, the proof of the pudding." The woman gestured her hand towards the stage, which was an open area at the other end of the room adorned with two chairs and a table.

The youth leaned over towards Dartey and put out his hand.

"I believe you must be Mr Dartey. I'm Henry Smith, Lili's brother. I recognised you from your photograph."

Dartey shook his hand and nodded, then quickly returned to study his programme. He had no idea what photograph the youth was talking about. Lili, he presumed, must be the girl. He had never known her name. His mother had interviewed

36

her when she first came from the agency and had not thought it necessary to pass on any information about her. Lili Smith. So now he knew her name. Lili. Lili Smith.

A dour, fat girl in jeans and a fisherman's sweater closed the door, pulled a black curtain across it and turned out all the lights. In the dark blankness Dartey had a moment of claustrophobia and an overwhelming desire to rush outside.

That was his first overwhelming desire; his second, after the girl appeared on the stage, was to drag her off it. Dartey was not a rescuer. He had always been one to let people stew in their own juice if they had chosen to do so. But this play was so patently bad, loosely structured, and totally uninvolving that it was a challenge to stay in his seat and watch the object of his affection be humiliated.

The woman who wrote it understood the people in it. The dialogue was faultless; it was as if she had tape recorded entire conversations. But putting a slice of life on stage was not gripping. Real life was boring. The play was boring. It made the girl appear boring. And the one thing Dartey had always felt about the girl was that she was not boring. He knew nothing about her but he sensed that.

Just before the end of the first act the girl did a dance. For seemingly no reason she took off her clothes and danced. He presumed that the dance was meant to express her torment because that was the main emotion that came across. Dartey felt embarrassed on her behalf although he had to admit that he was intrigued to see her naked body. It had, after all, been a desire of his for some time, but to see it in the company of all these sallow arty types was not quite what he wanted. He felt somewhat proprietary about her body. He had given it a great deal of thought of late and had made an emotional investment in it.

She was a skinny girl with no breasts to speak of, long thin legs and reddish pubic hair. She looked like a wild stick insect prancing around the room. He noticed that due to the boring nature of the play there had been much coughing and fidgeting after the first hour, exacerbated by the lack of air in this small back room. But when the girl began to undress there was total silence. It was as if everyone stopped breathing. There was no movement. It was extraordinary what effect nakedness had on a room full of clothed people. The girl was obviously not enjoying it though she did her best. She was gulping for air and her eyes had the hard stare of a caged animal.

She finished her dance. The lights went out and while she disappeared in the blackness the audience took a communal breath.

When the lights went on everyone rushed into the saloon bar and Dartey went with them listening for comments on the play. He caught, "Putney Bridge was a disaster as usual," and, "I parked right under a traffic light." No one mentioned the play.

He walked across the street, taking deep breaths of the cold damp air; he stopped to look in a fish and chip shop where an Indian couple were serving a long line of customers. A plump black girl sprinkled salt, pepper and vinegar over a steaming bag of chips and as she walked out, caught Dartey's eye.

"Want one?" she asked, proffering the bag of chips.

"Thank you." He selected the largest chip he could find. The girl walked away with two white girl friends who giggled and looked back over their shoulders as they went down the street.

He wondered if life seemed simple to them. A hungry belly. You fill it. Work. You do it. A man and a woman. They either mate or they don't. Sound anthropological principles which one read about in books. But he had met nothing but convolutions. Feeding hungry bellies meant destroying self reliance. Work caused corruption and decay. A man and a woman. Worked against their own self interest. Standing still seemed to be less destructive than going forward.

And this girl with her silly naked dance would rather he were not interested in her, that was quite clear. Who was he to say that it was not an extremely sensible attitude? Why was he going back to see her humiliate herself in that dreary back room? He had no idea. In that respect he was out of control.

The second act was mercifully short. After it was over most of the audience dashed out again into the saloon bar. The lady author leaned against the wall looking flushed and slightly paralysed. The youth in the wheelchair was talking to her at great length but she did not seem to be taking much of it in.

Dartey folded his programme carefully and placed it in his pocket. Lili Smith was the girl's name. Lili Smith. He walked towards the door and came face to face with Lili Smith. She was wearing a pale blue dress that she must have changed into with the speed of lightning. Her make-up was smudged around her eyes and for at least one second she seemed pleased to see him.

"Oh!" She gave him a slight smile.

He found himself examining the smudged eye make-up to see exactly where it had gone wrong. She looked at him waiting for him to say something.

"Why do you do this?" he asked. He was genuinely curious.

She looked first confused then utterly confounded by the question. She stared at him in a hard bitter way.

"Why do I do this?" She shrugged and walked away.

It was a simple question. Why was she doing this? There seemed to be no necessity for it and if there was one, perhaps she could explain it to him. Obviously it had been the wrong question as far as she was concerned. He watched her moving among the people left in the room, smiling a great deal as she talked and listened to the comments. She rarely smiled in his presence. He felt her awareness of him in that room but she did not look up at him once. After a few minutes he went into the bar, drank a quick beer and went home.

Help Me If You Can at the Actor's South Theatre is Eleanor Bright's first play and has many of the problems of a first play but is not without redemption.

The story (which begins a month before World War II breaks out) is simple. Hilda Bailey (played with spirit by Lili Smith) is a young wife and mother of two infants, whose husband is wrongfully accused of murder. Hilda makes every effort to save her man from the hangman's noose. In a meeting with the local Member of Parliament it becomes clear that he will make special efforts on her behalf in return for sexual favours. In desperation young Hilda submits. Before the M.P. can keep his part of the bargain, another man confesses to the murder and Hilda's husband is set free.

The husband Arthur (played with strength by Brian Argol) is distraught to discover what his wife has done. He goes off to the war, makes no attempt to shield himself from machine gun fire, and dies.

This is an old fashioned play with a modern twist. Director, Ian Harding, has devised odd interludes of music and dance which arrive unexpectedly.

The simple set was designed by Jeffrey Seed and lighting by P.D. Appleyard.

Dear Henry,

Can you believe this review? You can keep it if you like because I certainly won't. I think it's a classic example of un-think. He's managed to cover almost six column inches without committing himself to one critical thought. When in doubt tell the plot and give the credits. It's about as incisive as dish water. However, it's the first one we've had so I thought you might be interested.

I have now performed the play six times to the public. Ian decided that Act I was still too wordy so he's cut vast chunks of it. He goes a bit mad with his cutting and we have to prevent him from cavalier destruction of salient plot points. I think I'm bringing a little more humanity to the part. We have long arguments about whether Hilda is a victim. Ian of course sees her as a victim of capitalism, which is totally impossible to play. I see her as having chosen the role of victim, which is hardly any easier to play. It's no good being too objective.

And we still argue about the dance. He is as smug as anything about it. He was right, blah blah blah. It saved the play. Everybody talks about the dance. Someone phoned from the Daily Mirror etc. etc. I argue that just because they talk about it doesn't make it right. Being talked about is not the aim of the artist. The dance overwhelms the play. He discusses it in highly metaphysical terms but Jane (do you remember her? Stage manager, fat with bulbous nose) says that it's a tawdry peep show and I'm the poor sucker who's providing it. She's worked with Charlie before and she says that if he comes to see it he'll get drunk in the bar and then leap on top of me during the dance. So I'm not telling Charlie. As far as he's concerned I spend my evenings working at Spud-U-Like microwaving potatoes.

On a purely technical level I'm dancing better. I'm not so frigid with fear. I suppose you can get used to anything. They didn't give us nude classes at drama school but every actress I know ended up starkers eventually. If I ran a drama school I'd make everyone learn to walk around naked without flinching or twitching and then I'd teach them how to get an agent. There you cover two primary requirements. Drama schools are unrealistic havens, hell for introverts, bliss for show-offs. The only useful piece of advice I was given there was written on the exit door. PUSH.

I'm still fuming about Mr Dartey's comment. I'm fuming, one—because he said it, two—because he still doesn't realise why I'm fuming and why he shouldn't have said it. Why are you doing this? How could he ask me when I had just come off the stage? Doesn't he realise how incredibly vulnerable actors are when they've just finished a performance. I don't think we've said more than two words to each other since. And I certainly haven't been to any more of his lectures. I don't get paid for that. I was *astounded* that he came to see the play. There was quite a twitter back stage when everyone saw him come in; we all thought that even with the rather battered jacket and shabby trousers (or perhaps because of them) there was something of the laird or squire about him. And that amazing head might have been carved out of granite, so dark and brooding, it sets all the ladies' hearts athrob. Dark he definitely is but the brooding could be a pose. It may be a form of shyness. But one can't help thinking it's a sort of Byronic veneer. It's hard to imagine any substance there. I'm sure that he's had a very easy life and that his type of person is rolled out and produced with a pastry cutter. Public school, Oxford or Cambridge and then elegant service abroad. That's why his stupid little "Let them eat cake" type question really irritated me. I'm sure a performance in a grubby little pub seems ridiculous to him, but then he didn't have to come in the first place.

It's hard not to be bowled over by his sheer physical attractiveness, but not that hard. Who wants to worship the flesh? I don't want to be just another of his quivering fans.

Back to me and my play. I think we made the right decision not to tell the parents about it. The idea of them sitting there in the audience—well, it would just add fuel to their fire.

Keep the faith. Don't lose heart with your job hunting. Miracles do happen. Whoever thought I'd be working!

Love,
Lili

Dartey was losing patience. He would rape the damn girl and get it over and done with. The tension that had built up between them was ridiculous. It was hard to concentrate with her around: he could not get his work done.

But forcing himself on her would not work. He would have to try something more seductive. The only trouble was he did not know how to seduce a woman. In the past he had had a series of agreeable arrangements with women, almost man to man, no strings attached, and if there were strings he was off very quickly. He had not had to make any overtures. It was simply understood.

It was not even that he found her wildly sexually attractive. He did not have constant images of himself rolling around on top of her, penetrating her with great force. He did not have an erection the second she walked in the room. Admittedly the touch of her skin had been a shock, but that was probably something to do with the context of the scene. The boss unexpectedly touching the typist's hand. A fairly standard situation really. There was something very formal about the boss/typist roles and anything that broke through that formality caused a little frisson.

No, he simply wanted a response from her, an acknowledgement. But how to get it, that was the question.

There was no doubt about it that she had responded when their hands had touched, so perhaps what was needed was another accidental physical involvement. Perhaps he should trip over her and then knock her on the floor . . . He was getting childish.

Then again he could get another typist. That was possibly the simplest thing to do.

He sighed and looked over at the girl. Lili. She was typing as usual. That was all she ever did. She typed. She had given absolutely no indication that she wanted any kind of involvement with him. She was impenetrable. And obviously she was going to remain impenetrable.

Dear Henry,

Censored letter! Not for publication in biography.

Well. . . ! Mr Dartey stepped right out of character and made the most amazing commitment of energy and concentration unconnected with his work that I have ever witnessed.

He came over to my desk, took my hand, led me over to the couch, sat me down on it. Then he explained in a matter of fact sort of way that he was going to make love to me and that if I had any real objection, he would consider it, and that it probably couldn't make any difference because he was quite determined.

I always said that I would give in under such circumstances just to see what he looked like without a shirt on. But you know, I did have an objection. His great physical beauty is like an assault on one's senses. It's hard to relate to him as a human being. Also I felt like the parlour maid who had suddenly been favoured with the master's attention.

I explained the latter to him and he had the good grace to splutter over that and say it was nothing of the kind.

When you get very close to him, you see the lines on his face which give him a bit of humanity. He has quite deep frown lines, though what on earth he worries about I don't know.

He set about me in an apprehensive way, as though not sure if I were booby trapped. And just for a mini-second I felt rather sorry for him and . . . Well, need I go into the sordid details?

He didn't take his shirt off till afterwards when I asked him to remove it just for my sake. He's very brown and has a scar which I thought was from an African spear but it was from an appendix operation. The whole thing was a little nervous and furtive and I don't think I want to repeat it. I'm not sure my little typing job will bear the strain of this new turn of events.

I am considering my options, which are two. (1) Stay there and be open for further pillages and rapes from Mr Dartey. (2) Go back to the agency and ask for another morning job.

I still owe seventy pounds in back rent at my old flat, so I have to work somewhere.

I must admit being leaped on by Mr Dartey was not exactly a terrible ordeal, but it was a shock. I suppose one of the things that made it so unexpected was that we've never had a real conversation, just an odd spluttered sentence here and there. I'm beginning to think that he is simply a shy man who suddenly exploded.

It just occurred to me that Mr Dartey may have "got me out of his system" and it is merely vanity on my part to assume that he will lay a finger on me again. It is very unlikely that you will see a headline in a Sunday tabloid reading, "Typist Used As Sex Slave By Boss."

I am a little intimidated by the idea of looking for another job. I may have to really *work* hard in a new job and they may not appreciate my typing which has improved but is still not super slick. Although working for Mr Dartey pays poorly, he is the world's most lenient boss, to say the least.

Watch for the next exciting episode of the "Perils of Lili".

Love,
Lili

P.S. Do you think he will give me a raise now?

Dartey did not feel that either a friend or a lover was walking through the door when Lili arrived with a plain, unpermissive countenance the following morning. Her hair was drawn back off her thin face in an unbecoming style and she was wearing an amorphous navy blue cardigan that buttoned up tightly under her chin and appeared to be an impermeable barrier against any further invasion of passion. She was still very much the typist, who was willing in a thin lipped way to forgive and forget being pushed down on the couch yesterday.

One act of sex could not be counted on to make any great emotional transitions and in this case it had hardly dented the status quo. It was naive to think otherwise, but Dartey would have appreciated at least a small gleam of recognition in her eye.

He had, idiotically, rushed out and purchased six plates and a frying pan to go with the two cups and sole spoon in the kitchen. They were a sort of celebration of that one act of passion and he had hoped that she would notice them. They were also an indication to himself that he was planning to stay in London, at least until the end of summer.

As he watched Lili walk over to her typewriter and saw her thin frame etched against the vast airy expanses of grey carpet, he realized how empty the flat was. He made a mental note to do something about it.

Lili took the cover off her typewriter and went into the kitchen. This was her daily morning ritual. A good portion of her time was spent in making or drinking coffee. She would notice the new plates and frying pan; they were unavoidable in an otherwise bare kitchen. Dartey fought with the urge to follow her. He sat in his room and examined the ceiling for a few minutes. Then he attempted to compose a letter requesting tax deductible contributions to DAF.

When Lili came into the study to pick up her work, she had the expression of someone who didn't wish to be prevented from catching a bus.

He found himself saying, "Don't worry, I'm not going to tear your clothes off again."

"I'm not worried. I mean . . . I know you won't."

"You *know* I won't."

"Yes. I mean . . . Yes, I know you won't." She flushed a little and bent over the table to examine her forthcoming work with far more exactitude than usual.

"Is that a good thing or a bad thing?"

"Well it's . . . it was very pleasant but now we'd better . . . I know you want to get the work done."

"Pleasant?"

"Er . . . yes." She smiled politely, impersonally. Dartey shrugged and she made a quick, grateful exit.

He settled down to write:

Dear Friend,

I am writing on behalf of DAF's emergency relief efforts in Africa.

At this time Africa is suffering from the worst drought of the century. Twenty million people are now threatened with starvation because of the lack of rain and lower crop yields.

Dartey paused. It was accepted DAF policy to refer to the famine as a natural disaster. It had been, but was no longer his policy. Now he rarely used the word natural in reference to anything happening in Africa.

This disaster is one of the most compelling in our history, and will require gargantuan efforts to stop the human suffering. We need help to supply food, clothing and medical supplies.

All across the continent of Africa, where there has been a thirteen-year drought, the famine is out of control and will definitely get worse. I have seen mothers and babies dying in the hundreds and I have seen children no longer able to cry. I visited a food distribution camp which had run out of food, where an average of thirty three people died a day and where those with a little energy left foraged for leaves and insects.

46

I have visited Mozambique where it is reported that there were 100,000 deaths from starvation in 1983. We are half way through 1984 and the count is not yet in. There is still time to say starvation is preventable.

Dartey stopped. Was his letter already a touch too long? Don't give them MEGO was a well known axiom at DAF. MEGO stood for My Eyes Glaze Over and possible donors had to be protected from this mental switching off, which came after prolonged or frequent descriptions of suffering.

He had a UNICEF letter in his hand which stated that in the ten seconds it took the reader to open the letter, three children died from the effects of malnutrition somewhere in the world. After that the writer immediately described "four simple low cost techniques that could save the life of every malnourished child on earth."

Dartey admired that letter. He would try to imitate its splendid balance instead of writing one long angry wail. He crossed everything out and decided to return to it later.

Just before lunch the girl returned with her work and placed it on his desk. She scurried in and out of the room like an earwig that had had its large stone cover removed.

"Could you wait a second," he said just before she reached the door.

Dartey watched her as she hovered unwillingly. He was not quite sure what he had in mind.

He stood up, crossed the room slowly, and then grasped one of her wrists.

"What's wrong?" he asked.

"Nothing."

"That's good."

He took her other wrist, pulled her towards him and kissed her. She responded in the usual manner, politely. He glanced down at her wrists which had sustained deep red marks from his manhandling, excessively red, he thought. Obviously she had over-sensitive skin.

"You know, being compliant on all levels is not a requisite of this job."

She nodded, again politely. "Yes of course . . . I like this job. Well it's hard to find work nowadays."

"I wouldn't like to think I'm taking advantage of the unemployment situation."

"No you're not. Absolutely not."

Perhaps she was simply a boring young woman. Now they were having conversations she came out with nothing but trite remarks. It was an illusion that her eyes were wise and all-encompassing. She was what she was. Why should he expect her to be more?

He let go of her wrists.

"Right then!" He realized that he shouted that out like a military command.

He saw a glimmer of amusement in the girl's eyes that she quickly suppressed. She left quickly.

He had not behaved this stupidly since he was six years old and had been struck with the long blonde hair of a small girl at the riding stables. He had stolen some of his mother's jewellery and given it to her. She had accepted it like a merchant, examined it carefully for flaws, then put it in her pocket without saying thank you. He had even said, *"Please like me,"* a remark she had rightfully despised, and had trotted away on her small grey pony with her blonde hair bouncing tantalizingly on her shoulders.

The phone rang. It was Bert Hahn's secretary asking about the letter. Would he send it over this afternoon?

Dartey returned to his desk. Bert Hahn, DAF's executive director, would not sympathize with his current lack of concentration.

He would try a more detailed, incidental, approach. He wrote:

> Recently when I visited a black tent encampment in Foum Gleita, Mauritania, I met a man whose wife and two children had died of starvation. He was sitting staring at his feet. Scattered around him were the bones of dead cattle. He said he was praying to Allah for rain as only Allah could help now. He asked me why no one in the world seemed to care about them.

I am appealing to you as one who both knows and cares to make a donation to DAF so that we can bring food, medicine and clothing to these helpless people.

What next? Bert Hahn had said, "Keep it simple Dartey, because it is simple." Hahn understood one thing about Dartey: he found it difficult to be simple, therefore he was not a good company man. Dartey argued, Dartey philosophized, Dartey was a ruinously bad company man. Hahn had discovered this in the two short months that Dartey had been in London. There was no danger of his becoming the next executive director of DAF.

They had asked him to stay in London because they needed input from the field, but his input was filed away and had no effect on policy.

Bert Hahn had said, "Be a good chap Dartey and don't blame the lack of rainfall on neo-colonialism, and especially don't blame it on DAF." He was referring to a recent report by Dartey in which he had stated that it was likely that the drought in the Sahel was caused by governments, commercial enterprises and aid organizations who had pushed Africa into cash cropping and over grazing.

The resulting loss of vegetation reduced the soil's water storage capacity and this could be linked to reduced rainfall. The drought was therefore a recurring phenomenon and there was small hope for a return to former rainfall levels.

Pointing the finger of blame was not a useful contribution in a company where an atmosphere of guilt was considered unproductive and getting projects going was paramount. Asking Dartey to write this letter was a way of employing the delinquent child in a positive programme: get him to write a begging letter and perhaps he would start thinking like a company man.

Dartey poised his pen. In Africa he had the feeling that the continent was enclosed in another dimension where the facts never escaped. He would send back memos, warnings and advice which the head office ignored. He felt like a nomad standing on the cement-like earth in Mali where even the vultures had fled: he could cry out his need to the thorn bushes and the thorn bushes alone would wave back a sad response.

Now here he was in London and that feeling had not gone away, in fact it had increased.

He scratched out everything he had written and started again.

Dear Henry,

Life is extremely bizarre. After a week of poor audiences (one night just two people) this week has been considerably better.

A lot of it is just paper. Everyone's uncle and aunt has been given a free ticket, but some people are actually buying tickets and twice we have had a full house, that is thirty people crushed together on the folding chairs and four or five standing at the back.

Jane, the stage manager, says that a combination of nudity and social realism is irresistible. She says people can feel worthy and get a peep show at the same time.

It's certainly not the reviews that are bringing people in because so far we've only had that one noncommittal review in the local paper.

Ian has the absurd notion that he can get us transferred to a larger theatre and he never stops working towards that end. We are having a lot of extra rehearsals. If sheer will and effort could get us transferred, we would be in lights in Shaftesbury Avenue tomorrow. But poor Ian (Why do I say poor Ian? How could anyone feel sorry for that dogmatic, arrogant, manic tyrant?). "Poor" Ian has the enormous handicap of the play itself. The play seems to me like a skinny worm that has been encouraged out into the light of the hot sun and is shrivelling up under that dreadful light. It is a play that should have rested in a drawer in Birmingham.

However, to indulge myself in this opinion would sap my strength; so when I thrust myself out under the glare of that rather ineffectual shaking spotlight, I tell myself that there is genius in this play, but it will remain hidden if I don't interpret it. To the degree that I can believe that, my performance is good. And I will say this for Eleanor's writing, it may not be dramatic but it is never false. She understands people and reports their speech exactly.

As I write I'm realizing why Ian chose this play. It is an empty vessel for him to pour himself into. Every day he rearranges it, adds new elements, writes in dialogue, adds songs. We must have more music, he says, music touches on infinity, whereas words are earthbound. I think he means that the words in this particular case aren't good enough.

Last night he sat in the pub after hours drinking brandy and composing soulful songs. We all stayed for a while. Ian was busy writing and intermittently lecturing us on recognizing our homosexuality, but we had to leave at one o'clock because Brian drives everyone home and he was getting bored.

Ian stayed on and Mr Deakin, the proprietor, started to tell him about his World War II experiences. He had the job of picking up dead soldiers. Sometimes when there were too many to deal with individually he would pile them all together and set fire to them with petrol. He said that the world today was going crazy with violence and that he doesn't understand people anymore. I was being dragged out of the door by Brian then, but I would have liked to ask him what could possibly be more violent than his terrible war experiences. He talks about the war with a cheerful nostalgia but looks quite fearful when contemplating today's horrors. I suppose if young men were busy picking up dead soldiers nowadays they wouldn't be terrifying Mr Deakin. He might regard that as preferable.

All that talk of war and death seems to have infused itself into Ian's brandy sodden compositions. He wrote an absymal lyric to be sung to a tune highly reminiscent of "I know that my Redeemer liveth" with a jazzed up beat.

I see you as in a dream
You are not what you seem
You were once my life
But now there is nothing
Why me?

The pain is more than I can stand
Life is an abyss
I'm falling into

I keep on telling him that you can't finish the last line of a lyric with "into", but he won't listen. He thinks actresses are mental pygmies. "They can act intelligence, that's all. They're taught it in the third term at RADA."

Ian insists that this song will enlarge the scope of the second act. Brian will have to sing it. I'm glad I don't have to. I'm still suffering the agonies of the damned with my dance. Of course it does get a little easier. Embarrassment is not a chronic or growing emotion. It emerges, peaks, and then slowly self destructs. So the agonies lessen daily. I get to the theatre early before every performance to practise my dance. Jane always says, "Forget it. No one's going to notice your dancing technique."

My other news, rather inevitable really, is that I have been fired by Mr Dartey.

After the "large incident" on the sofa I was quite prepared to go on as if nothing had happened and be quite businesslike about the whole thing. But he was extremely tense and obviously expected something more, some sort of exegesis. But as far as I was concerned it was not very different from two rather enthusiastic dogs meeting in the park. They are certainly not torn by the necessity to make judgements about it.

I could feel that he wanted an acknowledgement from me that something had gone on, and I, for some perverse reason, just didn't want to acknowledge it. So I didn't. After all, we have yet to have a proper conversation. We never will have now.

I suppose I felt mistakenly safe in the assurance that he could not raise the energy to dismiss me. But he did.

He finally said, "Look here er . . ." He still doesn't know my name.

"Smith," I said. "Miss Smith."

This infuriated him.

"I think it would be best if you stopped working here."

"Oh."

"We seem to be at cross purposes."

"Yes perhaps we are."

He seemed very nervous and edgy and obviously could not wait for me to leave. I think he would have liked to push me out of the door but instead he jumped up from his desk and almost ran out.

I watched him go down the street and when he was out of sight I left too.

So my Dartey period is over. It has been two days now since I have worked for him. I'm going to miss that minuscule income I received but I'm not going to miss the dreary typing. I think I would miss the electric atmosphere and the heavy undulations of lust flowing from his room to my desk, were it not for my preoccupation with the play. The play diminishes the Mr Dartey drama, levels it flat really.

And as for Mr Dartey, I'm sure he'll get over the whole thing in a flash. In fact he's probably replaced me already with another female who might appreciate being thought provocative. I wonder if he picks his nose in front of her? He abandoned this practice in front of me as soon as he became aware of my existence. I realize now that this was very much the act of a suitor. I suppose I should have been more appreciative. It must have been quite a sacrifice for him.

I'm sorry your interview with the accountant didn't work out. It's amazing the excuses these people think up to avoid employing someone in a wheelchair. When I am rich and famous I will employ you as my accountant and recommend you to all my superstar friends.

Keep the faith.

Love,
Lili

The eyes of the world were on Africa. It had happened almost overnight. Dartey knew that the instant compassion that had been aroused would be emotional and short-lived but, like the

53

life of a butterfly, it would be flashy and magnificent in its short duration.

A trip to Africa with Bert Hahn was immediately arranged. Dartey was not looking forward to it. The charity business attracted a variety of odd bodies and Dartey had detected a certain degree of oddness in Bert Hahn, an oddness that went undetected or at least uncritized by anyone else at DAF.

Dartey had forgiven him his rushing off to Aquascutum to buy a Safari outfit. After all the man had to wear something. He had forgiven him his excitement. In a time of crisis those involved did get a certain charge, a contact high from a disaster; even a saint would be hard pressed not to feel it. No, that was forgiven.

It was Bert Hahn's undisguised relish he found unacceptable. Hahn positively glowed when he gave statements to the press and television. He was not troubled by the realization that the organization he was presiding over had poured millions of dollars and millions of man hours into Africa over the past twenty years and in that time Africa had grown steadily poorer and hungrier. The only cause that had been served, and grown stronger and more prosperous, was DAF. Their offices had sprouted up in cities all over the world.

Hahn would smooth his hair back and elegantly express his grave concern to reporters and television cameras. He was preening himself in the media spotlight. This was Dartey's interpretation of it: what others called articulateness and efficiency, rising to the special needs of the occasion, he called, "getting off on other people's suffering."

Dartey once attempted to voice this criticism to a co-worker who first agreed wholeheartedly and then accused Dartey of being hypercritical and indulging in the sort of picayune, schoolboy examination of motives that would result in paralysis.

What had brought Hahn his finest hour in this month of October 1984 was a six-minute documentary film on the famine in Ethiopia made by a British television crew. It was first shown on the six o'clock news and was quickly transmitted around the world. The heart-sickening pictures of starving children waiting to die, their small faces visited by flies that met no resistance, propelled the world into immediate action.

Dartey was stunned by the wonderful simplicity of the film and its instant grasping of the world's attention. The countless pleas, the desperate requests, the urgent memos which had been filed away and forgotten had suddenly found a champion in this small piece of film, which with one swift clean blow had cut through a thousand evasions and procrastinations.

His typewriter, the small machine he had been using to transmit his concerns, seemed a feeble, almost antediluvian means of communication. On his desk were dozens of sheets of paper covered in mere words describing exactly what had been shown on the film. The words had been without impact; he might as well have typed out knitting patterns.

He was doing his own typing now; he was a faster and more accurate typist than the girl. He experienced a sense of—if not peace, at least release without her there. Whatever it was it had been shattered by the film from Ethiopia.

If the film and its impact astounded Dartey, its contents did not. They gave him a dull sense of déjà vu. He had walked through those scenes in Wollo Province in 1973. He had watched a drought and famine undermine the people and depose the Emperor Haile Selassie. A famine that had been blamed on feudal elites and a three thousand-year-old dynasty was now repeating itself and discrediting a Marxist government.

He remembered his compound of musty tin and bamboo sheds in Wollo three miles from the one tarred road. It had been in better days a DAF vocational training centre. When it became a feeding station, thousands poured in and the government closed it down because it was attracting too many people. After pressure from Western countries, it was opened again. Hahn would probably take some pleasure in the rough living conditions, though he might not like waking up with dust in his mouth. He would certainly be struck by the spirit of grace and extraordinary beauty of the Ethiopian children and their madonna-like mothers, a beauty which never left them even when their skins sagged over their skeletal bodies and sad serene faces.

Two months after Dartey arrived in Wollo in '73, the summer rains came making the mountain roads muddy and impassable. Stories began to filter through of the great suffering experienced by those who could not reach the feeding stations. It was the end of the year before aid could get through but by that time it was too late. Two hundred thousand people died. They were buried under piles of stones which stretched out, as Dartey remembered, like mournful fingers towards the horizon.

At that time, eleven years ago, Bert Hahn had been in Norwich making millions out of manufacturing kitchen appliances. He had come late to philanthropy. Perhaps he was trying to purge himself of former excesses, too many champagne dinners and fancy sports cars; perhaps he was trying to wash them away in a sea of self denial. Whatever his original intentions, he had discovered that the goodness business brought its own pleasure. As far as Bert Hahn was concerned charity did not suffer long.

He reminded Dartey of a handsome pig. It was hard to imagine his plump pink face and thinning blonde hair withstanding the African sun. He would need a hat to cover the little balding spot. His well padded body would look more obscene than most in its constant comparison with stick-like figures.

"I love a challenge," he kept on saying. And who am I, thought Dartey, to say that he shouldn't be having a whale of a time. He'll probably enjoy his trip to Africa.

After the 1972–74 famine there had been a few years of respite. Then in 1982, after a long dry season, reports were sent to the UN Food and Agricultural Organization that the crops were failing in Ethiopia.

By then Dartey was in Lesotho battling with the realization that his best efforts only made things worse. It was his office to administer a goodwill that seemed to need genius or divine wisdom to be rightly placed. He and other expatriot dogooders had changed the fabric of village life in a more completely negative way then enemy occupiers. They had broken down family life, increased prostitution, set up a begging mentality in the children, all in the name of progress. The white man had rejected the material values at home and escaped to Africa. He then proceeded to inflict these same values on a black man whose way of life he could not assess because it was incomprehensible to him.

An old Basuto man told Dartey that the white man could never understand tribal custom because it was beyond his mental grasp.

So then, was no benevolence at all better than misguided benevolence? If it was, would it be the ultimate act of charity to simply remove himself?

He was still struggling with this question. He had spent fifteen years observing how charity blessed the giver but produced dubious results for the recipient. It was certainly blessing Bert Hahn. He had given his life over to good works and he was a happy man: he had bought his safari suit and he was ready.

In March 1984 the Ethiopian Relief Commission announced that millions of Ethiopians were in danger of dying of starvation. Relief agencies sent dire reports to their embassies where officials, who had no expertise in food supply, filed the reports away. They considered the reports exaggerated and anyway they had no desire to send sustenance to a Marxist regime.

But the film on the six o'clock news changed all that. The world woke up, including DAF where several hurried emergency meetings were held. Bert Hahn was called upon to make pronouncements about the disaster and to explain what DAF had been doing to avert it. Donations came in by the sackful. A seven-year-old girl in Luton sent her pocket money. A pensioner in Liverpool sent in ten pounds. A Bournemouth business man sent ten thousand pounds. Hahn hired several more secretaries to deal with the increased mail. Dartey noted with interest that they could type accurately and with great speed. Perhaps if the girl had been more efficient she would have been less visible and he would not have become preoccupied with her.

The girl. There was an ache inside him, a definite physical sensation, a misguided response to a non event. He was reacting to some delusion, not the actual facts about the girl. There had been a couple of times when he had a strong urge to stand outside the pub where she did that ridiculous dance and waylay her. But what would he say? She would stare at him in that icy way of hers and he would say nothing. No it was better that she had gone. He had some peace now and the urge to go racing after her would eventually go. It was not very different from giving up smoking. It would become easier as time went by.

Dear Lili,

Yesterday I was on the Central Line in the rush hour. It was a ridiculous time to travel with a wheelchair but I didn't have enough cash for a taxi and I had just come from a four thirty interview with a firm of accountants at Marble Arch. They were flabbergasted that I turned up and thought it was a gross deception. The receptionist said that I didn't sound handicapped on the phone but she became very evasive when I tried to pin her down on what a handicapped voice sounded like. I met a succession of individuals and they said ridiculous things like you won't be able to get up to the third floor and I said I was there wasn't I. They went on about fire emergencies and I challenged one of the guys to a race to the ground floor but he wouldn't take me on.

Anyway, in a very bad mood I hurtled my chariot down to the Central Line. I didn't want any help, I slid backwards down two flights of stairs and pulled my chair (folded of course) after me. I was banged on the head by copies of *The Standard* and plastic bags that must have been full of bricks. Finally two large American women, built like Japanese wrestlers, helped me the rest of the way, but they really slowed me down.

While I was sitting crunched on the train with one of my lady helpers practically sitting on my lap, I suddenly caught sight of your Mr Dartey looking decidedly glum about three crushed bodies away. I don't think he recognised me but I said hello, I was Lili Smith's brother and we had met at her first night. He seemed not exactly pleased at the sound of your name, more wary, as if I were asking him to jump into a pot of boiling oil. He pushed his way over to me and we had a sort of

58

conversation between Marble Arch and Oxford Circus.

He said he is going to Africa on Tuesday. I told him about your new job at the restaurant. He seemed to want details. He said he's been very busy and it's obviously taken effect. He has lost some of his gloss, he's a little faded. I think you left him just in time, although I must say my two Sumo wrestling ladies were eyeing him with great interest.

I thought you ought to know that the parents have got wind of your play. One of their swimming instructors has a daughter who knows your stage manager. I will try and hold them at bay.

Love,
Henry

P.S. Or could you possibly find it in yourself to come down and face them? It would make my life a lot easier.

Dartey was beginning to notice a new characteristic in his mother. She was anxious. It seemed to be connected to the impending retirement of the cook, Gabrielle, who was going to live with her sister in Baden Baden.

The threat of isolation after more than thirty years of companionship with Gabrielle led to certain modes of behaviour becoming more pronounced. Attitudes that were once cosy and motherly now emerged as strained and eccentric.

She offered advice. She had always offered advice, but now it was from a basis of fear. She would question him about his plan to visit Africa. The visit, according to her, was dangerous. Would he be on the phone? He explained that famine relief camps were not equipped with telephones, and that she had coped quite well with hardly a phone call over the past fifteen years.

She was worried about disease and war. The fear of death was in almost every sentence, which made conversation weighty and morbid. She advised her son to send Bert Hahn to Africa alone and type out instruction sheets for him which would eliminate the need for a guide.

At one point she even phoned Bert Hahn's secretary and had a rather senseless conversation about the forthcoming trip. Dartey restrained himself from getting angry with her but instructed her as forcibly as he could that if she had any concerns to keep them in the family.

The day before he caught the plane was a trying one. He had spent the afternoon persuading Bert Hahn not to travel first class and the evening assuring a doubtful Catherine that he was not going to die in Africa.

After leaving his mother just before midnight, he drove away with such a great sense of relief that it made him feel guilty. He took a deep breath and exhaled mightily trying to expel all that fear and cloying concern. Without realizing it he found himself driving through Notting Hill. It was almost as though he had blacked out and then woken to find himself cruising slowly along Westbourne Grove, coming to a stop outside the restaurant.

The fellow in the wheelchair had told him that the girl was working here at lunch times and on her night off from the theatre. It was Monday night and he knew that she had no performance. Not that he wanted to see her.

He would be quite satisfied with simply looking at the place. It had the appearance of a continental café with a tree-lined leafy patio festooned with fairy lights at the back. The sound of a singer accompanied by a guitar came up the stairs from the basement.

Perhaps he could get a glimpse of her without being noticed. It would be his consolation for the sheer discomfort he had gone through that day. No more than a glimpse though. A meeting, another of those incoherent conversations, would be a fittingly nasty capper to a dreary day.

He would not get out of the car, but just sit there for a minute and then drive away. He had not packed yet, though packing was hardly a compelling reason to leave. He would take very little. Having several changes of underwear seemed rather irrelevant in situations where people had nothing.

The music in the basement finished and was followed by a few cheers and some applause. Then the audience crowded up the stairs and emerged into the street. They were a motley group of young to middling, dressed in the baggy indeterminate style of the decade with only an assortment of jagged hair styles to give some definition.

It had started to rain. He watched every face to see if one of them belonged to the girl. There was a young woman with a mane of fluffy hair and a flowing black dress; instinctively he sank back into his seat trying to avoid her. But it was not the girl.

Then there was the girl. She came out of the door and paused to talk to a woman who was unpadlocking a bicycle. She stood in the rain under a street light, seemingly unconcerned about getting wet. Dartey began to feel as though he were in a cinema and she were on the screen. Thus he was invisible to her. He observed the curve of her cheek, washed clean by the rain of any artificial colour. Her skin was very white, picking up none of the yellow of the harsh street light.

The girl looked out across the pavement and saw him; she started and looked almost annoyed. He was not invisible after all. She said something to her friend who smiled and studied him with interest. The friend then mounted her bicycle and rode down the street leaving the girl standing there looking at him.

He should have driven away there and then, counted his losses and left. When he was on the plane the next morning, he could see that quite clearly. But there and then, with the girl standing under the street lamp, the rain drenching her hair into wet strings around her shoulders, he felt fixed and immobile, like a small rabbit in a headlight.

She walked over to the car and bent down. He wound the window down.

"What a coincidence," she said, "I was just telling Marianne that I worked on famine relief for four months."

He gave this some thought and then he said, "That must have been the consumption of the daily doughnut."

The girl blushed. It gave him the first sense of power he'd ever had in her presence.

"Would you like a lift?"

"No thanks. I have to go back and clear up."

Ignoring that, he said, "I won't attack you. I have a plane to catch in the morning."

She looked at him with a steady unfriendly gaze. "What's so anaesthetizing about catching a plane?"

He had an overwhelming desire to slap her hard across the face. His fingers twitched with the desire to lash out.

Instead he wound up the window and started the engine. She signalled for him to wind the window down, which he did, but only half way. It was a preventive measure.

"I'm sorry," she said.

"So am I."

He took one long hard look at her. Then he drove away.

Dear Henry,

The long Mr Dartey saga is over. I gather you must have given him exact directions to my restaurant, because he was waiting outside last night looking his most pathetic to date, like an old dog on a doorstep on a very cold night.

In turning down his offer of a lift I must have said one word too much, because it was almost as if he snapped in front of me and made a resolution not to take this bunk anymore. And as he moved off, just for an instant I felt sorry for him.

Up until now I've grudgingly admired his intellect but despised his great beauty and perfection. Feeling this sympathy was an entirely new sensation.

However, this does not augur a wondrous coming together in the best tradition of the woman's magazine serial because Mr Dartey is truly ticked off. I could see that I slowly disintegrated before him, changing from whatever he had constructed in his mind's eye to the incompetent typist that I had been originally. It was all in his eyes.

So the Dartey saga is over. If I want to continue to be the object of excessive devotion, I will have to find a substitute. Charlie is the obvious choice, but he can't avoid being base and would drown me in saliva.

You, my dear brother, may be called on to provide extra devotion until I have been weaned off the excessive dollop I've just had.

I will come down on Saturday morning. Please keep them at bay.

Love,
Lili

Henry was waiting at their old watching post in the entrance hall to the swimming pool when Lili arrived on Saturday morning. As she walked through the door she caught sight of him sitting on the floor wearing jeans and a bright yellow shirt. A stream of sunlight from a high and distant window illuminated his effervescent blond hair. They had spent a good portion of their childhood sitting on this spot, watching people pass by, questioning stoops and smiles and frowns, and causing some self-consciousness among those who caught the intense beam of their stares.

Several children trooped past on their way to a gala in the large pool. They shouted to make their voices echo against the old tile walls. The echoing sound and the smell of chlorine sickened Lili. It represented retribution for sins beyond her control, like retribution for breathing or eating. This archaic hall with its green tiles and crumbling ceiling where she had spent her childhood had now become a place where she gave an account of herself, where she paid up and made them feel that it was all worthwhile. They. Where were they?

"Where are they?" she asked.

Henry's eyes signalled upstairs.

"It's all right. I have them primed. They won't talk about anything except the weather."

Henry dropped off the packing case and propelled himself across the floor to the staircase leading up to their parents' flat. He pulled himself up the stairs with his large gnarled hands which smoothed out his journey like the metal belts on a tank.

Halfway up the stairs Henry paused, raising his torso and looking around, simulating the movement of a cobra about to strike.

"You didn't tell me that the DAF head office was near you." He looked at Lili accusingly. "I found it in the phone book. It's just off Ladbroke Grove."

"It hadn't occurred to me that it was important news." Lili kicked his feet, trying to make him move on.

"It's all in the interests of research."

"What research?"

"Information and background for your Dartey period."

"Dartey period! Look Henry, there wasn't a Dartey period. Let's get things in perspective."

"I'm the official biographer. You'll have to rely on my perspective."

"Henry! If you make something out of that I'll . . ." Lili's face flushed with annoyance.

"Break my knuckles? Kick me in the balls? What did you have in mind?"

A loud smoker's cough beckoned them from the other side of the door. Henry dropped down from his cobra position and led the way up to the door at the top of the stairs.

They went from the dark staircase to the living rom which was flooded with light, the freak bright light of the unusually potent November sunshine. The smell of chlorine had followed them up the stairs to this humid upper room, festooned with plants and the paperwork of swimming pool management.

Shirley, their mother, was sitting on her new white leather sofa with her back to the window like a casting director, smoking a cigarette and attempting to look reposed. Henry came in first, hauling his dead legs speedily across the floor and then pulling himself on to the sofa beside her.

Lili stood by the door noting that the only seat available was spotlighted by a bright shaft of sun, which would encourage microscopic observation.

Shirley removed her cigarette and examined her daughter who was still in a dark patch.

"Lili! Let's have a look at you . . ." She observed the long black dress, the hair that was no longer pink, the face that was no longer cadaverous.

"Normal. She looks normal," said Henry quickly.

"Yes, I suppose you could say that. Why are you wearing a black dress?"

Lili moved into the light, under the microscope, and sat down squinting a little.

"I bought it for work. It's better than lurex or jeans."

Shirley stubbed out her cigarette and groped for another one without taking her eyes off her daughter.

"Haven't you given that up yet? What about your health?" asked Lili.

"Health. Health. Hark who's talking about health." Shirley groped for her lighter and coughed. She did not look like a smoker: her track suit with the stripes down the side and tennis shoes gave her an athletic appearance and her black-grey hair was cropped in a sporty style. She had once out-run Lili in a race along the sand at Great Yarmouth.

"Your hair's not pink anymore. This is good. You can't get a job with pink hair."

Lili looked at Henry as some people look at dog owners with recalcitrant pets. Henry shrugged.

"Your father wants to see you. They're having a gala in the big pool this morning. He's trying to get away."

At that moment her father walked in. It was generally agreed that Roy Smith looked more like his wife than any other member of the family. When they were younger, they looked like an incestuous brother and sister. Now they were in their mid-fifties and Roy had spread out and lost the bird-like sharpness to his features, which Shirley had retained, and the similarity was less marked.

He stood in the doorway and looked at the back view of his daughter.

"Well thank God for that. The pink hair's gone."

He sat on the side of Lili's chair and put his arm around her. "And you've put some flesh on."

He studied her intently.

"Will you all please stop staring at me." Lili hunched herself down in the chair in an attempt to avoid the harsh spotlight from the window.

"You're an actress. You should like being stared at," said Roy.

"Not by people who don't pay."

"Get the kid some food," said Roy, pinching Lili's arm to test the thickness of her flesh.

"She's no kid, she's going to be an old lady. You'll be twenty-nine next Friday," said Shirley.

"I think you touched on these points before," said Lili giving another deadly look at Henry who shrugged helplessly again. "In fact, Henry said you'd promised to talk about nothing but the weather."

"Censorship," said Shirley drawing on her cigarette. "Do you expect me to say it looks like rain when my only daughter is being destroyed before my eyes?"

"This is not true," said Henry. "She's working, she has a roof over her head, and she's eating regularly."

"Yes. And it would be a real achievement if this was the middle ages; but this girl has a degree, she should be doing something with her life." In a moment of aberration Shirley removed her almost untouched cigarette from her lips and stubbed it out with a vicious concentration. "Joan Howard said that Jennifer's had a raise. She's getting twenty-five thousand pounds a year now. She has her own secretary and company car. And she was the girl who was always phoning and asking you to help her with her Latin homework."

Jennifer Howard was an albatross round Lili's neck. She had been an insignificant girl with plaits when they were at school but she had not remained insignificant. Now she was part of the package hurled at Lili every time she came home. She gave one more withering look at Henry and made a mental note never to come home again until she was rich and famous. This could be her last visit.

"I don't know why you're so impressed with wealth. You've never had any money. No one ever nagged you and made you feel guilty about it."

"I didn't have any education," said her mother.

"Education isn't necessarily the pathway to great riches you know. Education can teach you the redeeming value of poverty."

"We've all been redeemed enough in this house," said Roy. In matters relating to their children he was less intense than his wife. He was more ready to believe that if people wanted to ruin their lives they should be free to do so.

"I'm tired of being redeemed," said Shirley. "I remember when I first saw you in the hospital, I looked at this little red face and thought, this child won't suffer like me. You were a little ray of hope."

There was a silence in the room. Lili sank further into her chair and Henry studied the ceiling.

Finally Shirley said, "And now look at you. You look like death warmed up."

Roy stood up and rubbed his hands together positively. "Come on Shirl. She's looking a lot better. How about a cup of tea? I haven't got long. I'll have to go downstairs again in a minute."

"All I'm saying is she's an intelligent girl. There comes a time when you have to admit you've made a mistake. The acting thing isn't working out. She should use her education to get a good job, build a career for herself, especially if she isn't going to get married."

Lili stood up. "I think I'll go down and say hello to Bill. Is he on this morning?"

Shirley ran her fingers through her hair, stretched her arms in the air to show finality. "You don't have to escape, that's it. I've had my say."

"Right. O.K.," said Lili and slipped out of the door.

There were two pools at the Berkeley Road Swimming Baths. The larger one was currently being used for a school gala and the shrieks of the swimmers and spectators echoed throughout the long tiled hallways. The baths had been built in 1906, with private baths for those with no bathrooms, and a myriad of subterranean passages and small rooms Lili used to explore as a child. Since the local council's decision to pull the baths down, an air of neglect and letting go had pervaded. The green paint, always green, was peeling, the tiles were chipped and graffiti was beginning to creep along the walls like a rampant disease.

In the small pool, which was generally used by inexperienced swimmers and small children, all the Saturday morning swimmers were crowded together, indignant at their expulsion from the large pool. Groups of wet and shivering children, with mottled mauve and white legs, were huddled on the side.

Lili knew that these children might be shivering but they did not feel cold: children ignored the word cold, it was not part of their vocabulary. She had stood there coloured with those same mauve and white striations, she had dived in with all those pubescent bodies, uniformly smooth, like slithering tadpoles; her eyes fixed on the cracked green tiles and the electric clock from Woolworth's that her mother had put up to replace a more worthy but defunct Edwardian antique. The clock was still there, its red plastic casing looking pitted and bent, but still there, despite frequent arguments with the council about its unsuitability, not being standard swimming pool issue. Lili's swimming days were intense, the water was always there, the nice exhaustion, the engulfing wetness, the increasing speed; all this had not prepared her for the sporadic movement and dereliction of her theatrical career.

Bill was there, still old but not older, he had always been old. He was sitting on an upturned bucket, his florid unlined face with its frame of bushy white hair, frowning over the sports page of the *Daily Mirror*.

"Hello Bill." Lili felt stupidly emotional as tears came to her eyes, misplaced tears. She had to cry over somebody, so she was crying over Bill and his old bucket.

Bill looked up. "Well look who's here." He folded his newspaper and slipped it into his pocket. "Are you a star yet?"

"Oh don't you start."

"Well it's a mug's game. I read about those stars in the paper. They're all miserable as sin."

"They probably weren't looking for happiness in the first place. I'm certainly not."

Bill tapped the side of his bucket and cast his eye over the tangled mass of bodies in the overcrowded pool.

'Your ma tells me you're working in a pub for nothing."

Lili stared fixedly into the water until the blue of the water and the odd shapes of the swimmers became a kaleidoscope pattern.

In that mosaic of water and bodies she seemed to see Mr

Dartey doing a lively front crawl, obscuring the rare blue patches of water with his muscular frame; then his body seemed to immobilize and freeze, reverting to the image she had always had of him, the impeccably handsome model in the glossy magazine. She shuddered with distaste.

Turning to Bill she said, "I am getting paid."

Bill nodded approvingly and tapped the side of his bucket. He observed a boy dive bombing into a mass of bobbing heads and blew his whistle when the offending party was under the water and could not hear it. She wished that she could find something as engulfing as water to protect her from similar invasions.

On her way back upstairs Lili ran into Mrs Wright, the cleaner, who was polishing the brass knobs on the front doors. She belonged to the old school of cleaning ladies who believed in constant vigorous motion and felt a loss of self worth if they stood still. Years ago she had looked like a caricature of a cleaner with her hair tied up in a scarf and a front tooth missing. But she had moved into the eighties with style, having her hair permed, dentures fitted, and a bathroom built next to her kitchen. She had originally taken the job at the swimming pool because she could take a free bath every Monday. Now that she had a bathroom of her own she stayed on because she could not break the habit.

"Hello stranger," she said to Lili. "How's the life up in London? Got a job in a film yet?"

"No, not exactly."

"Then why bother with it? There's no point in suffering if you don't have to."

"That's very true Mrs Wright." They had all been brainwashed by her mother.

As she walked slowly up the stairs to her parents' front door she became aware of her mother standing in the shadows on the top step. She could see the light of her cigarette flashing like a disapproving glow worm.

A sudden reflex action made Lili stop and half turn back.

"Don't be frightened. I'm only your mother."

"Why of course, warm fires, soft bosoms, gentle hugs. How could I not recognize it?"

"I can't keep quiet, I'm sorry. You'll be thirty next year. Somebody has to make you wake up."

"I'm an actress. It's what I do. It's what I'm trained for. I'm an actress."

"No you're not. An actress is somebody who acts. You're dancing in a pub with nothing on and you're not getting paid for it. You only think about acting."

"Then it's the only thing I can think about. I don't want to change. I can't change. It's like asking me to stop breathing. And anyway I am getting paid."

Roy put his head around the door. "Come on girls, I've made tea."

Lili ran past her mother like somebody trying to get away from a sudden down-pour. But Shirley followed her fast behind.

"And I know you Lili. Even if you become a star you'd be bored with it in a minute. It's just a dangling carrot to you, that's all."

When they were inside Roy shut the door and beamed reassuringly like a kindergarten teacher: it was his way of dealing with a family "atmosphere".

He poured out tea and changed the subject. The spotlight was taken off Lili and they discussed the closing down of the swimming pool and Henry's job applications. Lili felt an unspoken criticism in the obvious comparison between her and Henry. Here he was seeking respectable employment and showing a commonplace maturity which seemed entirely out of her grasp.

Henry came with her to the station to say goodbye. He continued to discuss the location of the DAF headquarters. Lili decided that the best tack was to hide her alarm and to be non-committal. Perhaps this was the best way to make him forget about it.

As he was in the middle of explaining that he had looked it up in his A–Z map, Lili's train came in and she raced off down the stairs to the platform leaving Henry to shout that the DAF office was in a mews directly under the Westway.

Lili was pursued by Mr Dartey on the way home. He was standing on the platform at Clapham Junction and she saw him disappear into the crowd at Victoria. She saw him again in an adjoining carriage on the Circle Line. On each occasion when his face turned towards her and she realized it was not him, she felt foolish for having interpreted a dark head of hair or a certain shape of the forehead as being the likeness of Mr Dartey.

Perhaps Mr Dartey had ridded himself of his obsession and dropped it, as though it were a solid object, into her lap.

Or, more realistically, Henry would not let the subject die, with the result that she was seeing Mr Dartey in every man. Henry would soon grow tired of it, just as she had.

Part Two

By the time they reached Mali and were driving erratically over the potholes of Bamako, Dartey and Bert Hahn had been travelling together for a week. They were woefully incongruous partners but were not without the desire on either side to make the thing work. Dartey managed to harbour no criticism about Hahn's constant need to find a phone, his entire day being organized around a call to his wife.

Hahn, on his part, did not criticize or even remark upon Dartey's subtle racial prejudice. He observed how Dartey seemed to relax among Africans and relate to them on a mystic level as an honorary African, a level reserved for them alone and excluded from non-African DAF workers. Hahn, as one of the white pariahs, treated this as a challenge; like Will Rogers, he had never met a man he didn't like and looked on Dartey as an interesting case.

Neither was Hahn defeated by his own small acquaintance with Africa. He had visited the place several times, it was true, but knew little more than an enlightened tourist. To further his knowledge he had no compunction in asking everyone's opinion, much to the amusement of Dartey. He had received advice on how to run DAF from a Mauritanian waiter, a Senegalese driver and a street vendor in Bamako, not to mention countless abandoned refugees who poured out ideas on how they could be better served.

Hahn was a complete believer in the "trickle down" philosophy. He was only too familiar with the development versus no development debate: he found the argument for leaving Africa to the Africans simplistic. "We live in the twentieth century," was how he would deal with that. Dartey in his dispatches in recent years had been the chief chronicler for DAF of the disastrous outcome of incompetent aid. To Hahn he seemed like a voice of doom that almost revelled in doom for its own sake.

Dartey belonged to a growing school of Africa watchers who warned that the entire continent was falling apart because well-intentioned white men aided and abetted by black governments were crushing it under a welter of ill conceived programmes until there was nothing left for Africa to do but slowly die. He wrote passionate pieces on soil erosion and its drastic consequences, citing the Islands of Cape Verde west of Senegal as an example of what might happen to the rest of Africa; in the Republic of Cape Verde soil erosion was so far advanced that some experts were considering that the islands might have to be abandoned and thus, said Dartey, might go the rest of Africa.

Hahn had read the dispatches on Cape Verde and given it to his secretary saying, "Our man Dartey is suggesting that Africa may have to be abandoned in the not too distant future." He made some good jokes around the office about Dartey organizing a full scale exodus from Africa and wrote a witty memo about research into methods used by Noah.

On other occasions Dartey had written long and detailed letters to headquarters advising them not to send large amounts of grain when it was not direly needed. He cited the example of Gambia: the United States of America sent vast quantities of unrequested grain to this country which had withstood the 1973 famine and relied on its own ample crops. Aid of this kind, he said, had a similar effect to a hostile invasion, it reduced incentive and increased dependence.

During the 1973 famine Dartey had frequently advised that more attention should be given to distributing home grown crops in the six drought stricken countries: he claimed there was more food available in these countries than people were aware of. This was before Hahn had started work at DAF but on his arrival he was soon made aware of the fact that Dartey argued for less rather than more. Hahn considered that this argument taken to its ultimate conclusion would lead to the dissolution of DAF and the dissolution of himself. He dismissed such arguments as impractical, mere rhetoric like most socialist ramblings, a backdrop of words while he got on with the real business of running DAF.

"There are starving people here, we'll do our damndest to feed them," was Hahn's way of dealing with Dartey's complex debates on whether or not every DAF worker in Mali was increasing desertification.

In Bamako Dartey had pointed out that an entire suburb had arisen during the '73 drought to house the experts who had arrived to roll back the desert and prevent Mali from suffering from famine ever again. The houses were furnished with well-stocked kitchens and stood as monuments to the previous famine and Dartey was sure that more would be built as monuments to the present one, while the desert continued its inexorable march south.

On the first morning there they had drunk strong French coffee, eaten freshly baked croissants and glanced at a copy of *Le Monde* like Parisian businessmen or as Dartey remarked, "Like well paid employees of the drought industry," and then they set off for the north.

Dartey was disconcerted to find that he had brought the girl with him; he had assumed or rather hoped that distance would dismiss her, that in the expanse of this great continent her presence would be minimized and then disappear completely. But she was a live, physical presence still, an uncomfortable burden that made each day and each night pressured. He remembered the unearthly softness of her skin, an extreme contrast to the brittleness of her manner. What could he have done to make her smile? He felt like a silly dog tied outside a supermarket yearning for an uncaring owner. The girl had become an uncomfortable rash, a blight that he was completely willing to dismiss but could not; he found her presence inappropriate at this time, an erroneous distraction from the task at hand. But there she was. She was there.

He managed to momentarily dismiss her as they drove in an ancient Ford truck along roads which were usually bordered with trees and grasses at this time of year, the end of the so-called rainy season: but now the roadsides were dry and dusty. The trees were dying, giving way to the desert. Sixteen years of drought had sent the desert sands spreading southwards like an incoming tide. A way of life was being destroyed as nomadic tribesmen who had driven their camels across the Sahara for centuries had been forced to take refuge in Mopti, Gau and Timbuktu.

There was a new term for them, a phrase for the eighties, ecological refugees. They had been categorized and filed away as the Sahara had taken over their country and turned it into a dusty lunar landscape. Further west, Mauritania was blowing into the Atlantic Ocean according to an American television correspondent they met in Toni, a little American hyperbole, Dartey thought, but not too remote from the truth. Nouakchott was almost engulfed by sand dunes, a sad fate for a capital city. A green belt of plants and shrubs was being planted to serve as a living shield against the city's most ruthless invader in a thousand years.

A television correspondent was almost as rare as rain, for the media, with a few exceptions, had not yet discovered the famine in Mali. They were fully occupied elsewhere, jostling for position among the film stars and politicians at the airport in Addis Ababa.

Mali by contrast was unvisited and very quiet. Dartey considered Hahn and himself poor substitutes for celebrities, especially since Hahn had taken to vomiting and having sudden attacks of diarrhoea at unexpected moments. It entailed many quick sorties to or behind whatever was available, depending upon the sophistication of the surroundings. Trees, Hahn discovered, disappeared in exact proportion to his dire need of them.

The situation there had deteriorated since Dartey had made a brief visit in April on his way back to London. There were more people going hungry and they were in a worse condition. He photographed two exquisite little Tuareg children, a boy of eight and a girl of eleven, who stared through and beyond the camera to the distant horizon. The beauty of their young faces had not yet been touched by malnutrition, fine perfectly proportioned heads and eyes not yet dulled gave the appearance

78

of a radiant normality. Only the protruding veins on the young girl's hand and the exaggerated boniness of the knees were the marks of famine.

The children were part of a group of twenty or so Tuaregs who were on their way to Mopti which was another forty-five miles away. There was little Dartey could do for them except give them directions to a DAF clinic and distribution centre where they could get medical attention and, he hoped, food.

There was a problem with food delivery and the DAF workers they had met so far were moving beyond frustration into cynicism and lethargy. Previously the government had kept the consignments of food that DAF sent to them and not distributed them as agreed. Now DAF had changed its policy and sent food directly to the DAF centres but the cargoes had been held up at the ports and still were not reaching the hungry.

At one time Dartey had argued for sending money directly to those in need to purchase food from the local markets. He felt that the possible inflation in prices due to the sudden influx of large sums of money on the market would be balanced by its usefulness in stemming the tide of starvation. But recently he had concluded that this method was as counter-productive as any other.

Years ago he used to visit an old man who was born during the empire of Samory. The man told him, "We don't need your charity or your greed. We want the respect that is due to us and this will open up the channels that we need."

The old man had long since died but Dartey thought of him as he made his way across arid stretches of Mali. The beauty and secret strength of Mali, though severely battered, still held an enduring fascination for Dartey, and demanded respect. He felt the imposing presence of the medieval empire of Mali, a great and powerful state with incalculable coffers of gold in its majestic palaces. When the great emperor Mansu Musa made his famous pilgrimage to Mecca in 1324, his fabled city of Timbuktu was an important centre of trade and scholarship. The subsequent invasions by the Moroccans, the Tuaregs, the Fulani and the French had been more than equalled, as far as

Dartey was concerned, by the international aid and development organizations in shattering Mali's spirit and confounding the effects of drought.

Dartey had hoped that by the time he had criss-crossed Mali and visited every woebegone DAF worker that he would have exorcized the presence of the girl. But she remained with him. In pondering the farcical relationship between them he concluded that he had been vulnerable to her because he was in London, which had become a foreign city to him. He felt a little more sane here, even in the insanity of the famine. With increasing sanity would come the return of reason, and with reason she could be banished, obliterated.

Dear Lili,

Did you know there was a small paragraph in yesterday's *Standard* saying that your play will be going into the West End in January. Producer Jonathan Black thought it "a little gem of a play" with some "poignant musical moments".

Can this be the same play?

Love,
Henry

Dear Henry,

We all confronted Ian with the article in the paper. He said he was planning to contact our agents tomorrow. I expressed the opinion that as he hangs around the theatre every night it would not have taken an enormous effort to open his mouth and tell us. After all it was fairly earth shattering news.

He seemed very calm about the whole thing. It had "only been a matter of time before it transferred", it was a "simple natural progression and what else did you expect".

Of course if I'd have given it any thought I would have

predicted this typically pompous reaction. It was naive to expect anything ordinary and human from him.

On the other hand we underlings are all overwhelmed. We had no idea how he did it or what sort of transaction went on, but we are astounded.

Jane, who is the only other one reacting like Ian, said it was not that surprising since he had hedged his bet by turning it into a nudie musical. She told us that she had already wangled herself into stage managing the West End production but not to keep our hopes up because he would dump us and get some stars.

If Jane is right, I will be out of a job soon and there is little hope of an obscure underpaid naked actress becoming a well known, well paid one!

Love,
Lili

P.S. In the paper today I saw a picture of Bert Hahn (the head man at DAF U.K.) taken somewhere in the Sahel. He was holding a tiny emaciated baby on his large fat thigh. I studied the picture carefully to see if there was a piece of Mr Dartey in the background but there was nothing except dozens of skeletal people.

For a good two minutes the picture made Ian and the play fall into perspective.

Getting back to his old haunts must have been like a douse of cold water for Mr Dartey. I'm sure he's forgotten me.

On Thursday 13th December they arrived in Chad which, according to the World Bank, was the world's poorest nation. Poverty seemed to encourage vulgar displays by Bert Hahn. On his first morning there he donned a Gucci belt and a gaudy pair of sunglasses with thick gold frames studded with paste diamonds that caught the sunlight and sent out iridescent rays. Their driver, a talkative ex-soldier who was wounded in the civil war, watched the flashy movement of the sunglasses as a cat watches a ball of string.

"I make you an offer," he said frequently to Hahn, who would nod seriously as though considering it but did nothing about it. It would seem that Hahn's preoccupation with the workings of his bowels made him absent minded.

Though Chad was twice the size of France there had not been more than forty-eight miles of paved road since Dartey had first travelled through the country fifteen years before. Driving around was bumpy to say the least and had a disturbing effect on Hahn's condition, causing many quick evacuations of the car.

The Logone river in N'Djamena was almost dried up and the Chari River had shrunk drastically; their talkative driver took them to a point where the bounteous Chari was once six hundred yards across and was now little more than one hundred yards. They drove up to Lake Chad and found that the gigantic lake which bordered four countries was now eighty per cent dried cracked earth.

Many of the people there had no food except what they received from aid and getting it to them seemed almost impossible. The Nigerian leader General Muhammed Buhari had refused access to relief shipments. Although no reason was given, Dartey suspected that Buhari was still nursing a resentment against the people of Chad because of injuries he received while fighting there years ago. Dartey arranged for DAF supplies to go instead through Douala in the Cameroon.

Hahn was not coping well with the daily viewing of the African holocaust. He had gained almost ten years in just under three weeks, a combination of the depressing sights and his rapid loss of weight. Though appearing older he still had sufficient padding to prevent any gauntness.

The Sahel had quickly chastened and diminished Hahn but he managed to produce a flash of his old managerial self when he learned that deliveries going through the port of Douala would take four weeks instead of the desired six days from Lagos. He spent an hour on the phone berating any Nigerian official who would stay on the phone long enough to be insulted and abused. It seemed to help Hahn. Dartey considered it better but no more productive than banging his head against the wall.

Dartey realized one night as he retired to an airless room in N'Djamena that he had had his thirty-eighth birthday ten days before in Mali. He felt old, very old, and subject to all the concomitant weaknesses of age.

Perhaps he had attacked the girl in London because he was trying to prove himself; perhaps he was like plump middle-aged Hahn who lit up like a beacon around any pretty girl.

Whatever it was he wanted to overcome it. And, he decided, that determination to overcome it was the first step towards it, towards becoming himself again.

Dear Henry,

I learned only fractionally before the new cast list appeared in *The Stage* that I am the only person from the original production still in the play.

We are all reasonable actors and there was no reason to eliminate anyone. I would love to say that I outshone everyone else but it simply is not true. I had the largest role and that was about it. If they were to replace anyone, it should be me.

I naively tried to get an honest explanation out of Ian. He said they had talked to several stars but could find no one with a "less confrontational body".

I have attempted to analyze the obvious implications and tried to see what twisted meaning is lying underneath but have drawn a blank.

The only thing I can come up with is that if he had put a star in my part, he would not have been able to manipulate her to such a degree. Ian, I've now discovered, is manifesting the bully/coward syndrome. As my part holds the key to the play, he is probably fearful that if he had to kowtow to a well established theatrical star the play might slip from his grasp.

I am going to get £131·18p per week (West End minimum). Jeffrey (my silent and invisible agent) couldn't get any more out of the producer because I'm unknown and a risk. When the producer came to see the play in Clapham he said I was "absolutely solid" which I think was a compliment but obviously does not translate into money.

Charlie read the announcement in *The Stage* and is furious that I've been holding out on him.

"Why didn't you tell me," he keeps on saying with a genuinely hurt expression, "after we've been living together all this time?"

I have given up trying to correct the impression held by all Charlie's friends that we're lovers. I'm sure he concocts some fascinating details for them. He is absolutely unsquelchable and still tries his nightly lunge. Last week I had to punch him hard on the nose before he would get off. He says that I've saved him from the worst excesses of the mid-life crisis. I think he means that my presence in the house gives him something to talk about and infuriates his ex-wife. Though it has not saved him completely.

He mourns for his life so much, sometimes I think he's going to cry. All his money is going on alimony and child support. He's just had his forty-sixth birthday and he's been out of work for three months. With his white-blonde hair and eyebrows and pink face (getting redder from too much alcohol) he looks like a tinted negative.

My transfer to the West End has made him both delighted and jealous. He sees it as an amazing triumph but why can't he get a nice steady stint in London too?

The new actors and I are rehearsing in a hall off the Tottenham Court road. The play seems lost in this larger setting and makes me uncomfortable. I feel like an animal who has been kept trapped in a box for so long that when it is set free it wishes to return to the safety of the box.

I thought that well known actors would be better than unknown ones. So far this does not seem to be the case, but I will withhold comments for awhile. Do you know David McNair? He's playing my husband and he's—well he's theatrical. I will bide my time and watch.

Our author, Eleanor, came down from Birmingham to see the first run-through and did not recognize her play. Ian handled her in his usual cunning, placatory way and persuaded her that he has changed it along the lines she would have done if she were there!

Being a total novice, she has no idea where she stands or what she can do to protect her play. She doesn't know what to say to Ian and she stands there like a mother watching her small child go off for its first day at a particularly nasty school.

She did say to me at one point, having watched all the songs and dances, "It's like *South Pacific*!"

She said her husband is getting resentful at all the time she is spending down in London. He's giving the children sausages and chips every night and she's worrying about their getting clogged up with grease.

Ian looks like the cat who's swallowed the canary. Apparently he used his own money for the production at *The Princess Louise* and now it's beginning to pay off. His anxiety to protect his investment is producing, if possible, even more manic behaviour. However, his channels to express it have been considerably reduced now we have a new cast. He's a real Uriah Heep with the stars, listens to their opinions and smiles and makes jokes with them. He vents his spleen on the stage management and me: we are his collective cat that he kicks frequently. We sometimes get together and plot a variety of painful deaths for him. Jane has some amazing ideas.

While Eleanor was away, he announced that he had managed, by Herculean efforts, to give a play that was once just an extended beginning a firm structure with a beginning, middle and end. In my opinion it is still an extended beginning with a few songs and dances added. There is a story, well you know, you've seen it, but it is just a series of conversations. When the husband dies at the end, it is dealt with in such an unclimactic way that you feel something else must happen, but it doesn't. I'm sure Eleanor has deep feelings about the story and a reason for wanting to present it but she does not have the skill to communicate it.

I am not going to panic if the parents come to the first night. After all things couldn't be worse with them than they already are.

Love,
Lili

85

Dear Lili,

The parents *are* coming to the first night, so am I. I'm renting an incredible suit and fluffy pink shirt. I will be glistening in the stalls.

I went up to London yesterday with Bill in his van. He was picking up some tyres from his brother in Hammersmith. At my request we drove down to Ladbroke Grove and looked at the DAF U.K. head office. It is in a rather isolated mews by the Westway and the Metropolitan railway line, an island of trendiness in a sea of grot. DAF owns a building that seems to be part of the creeping grunge that has slipped in from outside, peeling paint, two broken windows replaced with paper etc. They are a real betrayal of the upmarket image of the houses around it and material evidence that DAF funds are not being frittered away on comfortable offices.

I will report further developments in this area.

Love from
Henry

By Wednesday 26th December Bert Hahn and Dartey were travelling along a road leading to Tekl El Bab in the Sudan. Their car moved swiftly along a straggling line of refugees and engulfed them in a cloud of dust, a graphic example, thought Dartey of the mission of mercy becoming unmerciful.

When the car stopped and the dust settled there was little to see from one horizon to the next except the jebel, or giant rock, some miles away at Tekl El Bab, and close at hand the dead eyes and tattered rags of the fragile stick-like figures of those who had been travelling for weeks from Ethiopia. There seemed to be a hundred tales of personal tragedy and families divided but Dartey, like most men unable to absorb too many individual disasters, picked out one man. He noticed a handsome Tigrean walking mechanically along the roadside in the slightly mesmerized way of people who have walked for many days. The man carried a small limp body. The body was that of a girl of perhaps seven or eight years old: she hung face downwards over his arm like a limp doll dressed in a few soiled rags. The man supported her scrawny buttocks with his other arm and did not look at her as he walked. Dartey thought she was dead and wondered why the poor man struggled along the roadside with this dusty corpse until he noticed a slight movement of the child's hand,which she drew slowly and gracefully up to her forehead as though trying to alleviate a headache. It was an incongruous movement. It was a motion often made by his mother when she would sigh and say, "I've had an exhausting day!"

At Dartey's request the man stopped. The child returned to her motionless state and hung like an old coat over the man's arm as he watched the car's trail of dust settle. Speaking in a low husky voice the man told them that his name was Berhanu and that he had walked two hundred miles. His crops had failed and his wife and two other children had died on the journey. Most of the time he had been forced to walk at night because of Ethiopian air attacks.

Hahn understood nothing of the conversation conducted in an alien tongue but nevertheless he joined in. He offered Berhanu a lift in loud English with many gesticulations which did nothing except disturb him. After a minute or two of staring distrustfully at the car and the driver, who was wearing an old military uniform, Berhanu climbed into the back seat of the car. The driver, for his part, looked at him no differently than any taxi driver would look at an extremely dusty and lice ridden passenger. Dartey had taken the child and found her lighter than a skeleton, as though even her bones had been drained of any substance, and all that was left was skin and air. Her name, her father told them, was Zabish.

In the car Dartey gave Zabish some water which she had some difficulty in swallowing. The water trickled down the side of her face and on to her neck creating little shiny pathways along her dusty skin. Her eyes stared past Dartey as though he were non-existent and up to the roof of the car which seemed to hold some reality for her.

When they arrived at Tekl El Bab they found no kind of an oasis. There was no water, food or sanitary facilities. Between thirty and forty thousand men, women and children were crouching under thorn bushes covered with palm leaf mats or strips of canvas; others were sheltering among the boulders of the jebel which stretched up a thousand feet into the sky and cast its shadow over this barren strip of desert.

Dartey discovered that the food had run out several days before. Some relief workers had set out to bring food and water from other camps but had not yet returned and there was little for any one to do but wait. Dartey found no DAF workers there apart from a nurse who had worked briefly for DAF in the past and had arrived at Tekl El Bab under her own volition. She sat in a roughly assembled tent holding a dying baby and complained bitterly about the lack of medicine and facilities.

It took very little time to discover that there was no organization, that nobody knew what anyone else was doing. The only consistent reality was the expanding graveyard of freshly dug graves which lay outside the camp.

Dartey and Hahn had left Berhanu and Zabish by the makeshift clinic. After an hour of touring the camp Hahn suddenly stopped.

"We'll have to take Berhanu and his child back to Kassala. That girl's going to die here," he announced in a voice filled with panic as though he were talking about his own daughter.

Dartey studied him for a moment. Hahn was sweating and out of breath, his face was red and swollen from too much sun and thin streaks of damp blond hair stuck to his forehead. Dartey restrained himself from saying the obvious. He simply followed Hahn.

He was amazed to find himself following this great perspiring, porcine man in an aimless search. Berhanu and his daughter were not where they had left them and had obviously sought shelter from the midday sun under a bush or boulder and had blended in with the thirty thousand or so other individuals. If he were searching for a needle in a haystack, Dartey concluded that he would have jumped all over the hay with his bare feet until they were pierced by something sharp and metallic; but here in the human maze of this smelly, disease ridden camp he could not think of a similar solution.

He bent down and peered into one family group after another. Everywhere was the ceaseless wailing of sick and hungry children, a sort of sad chorus that never left them. They were accompanied in their search by a band of children who were not yet wailing. Some held Hahn's plump damp hand and others gripped Dartey's relatively cool dry one, gazing up expectantly into their eyes as though these men, if not harbingers of salvation, would at least provide an interesting afternoon.

Then suddenly Hahn dived between two boulders at the foot of the jebel and came back holding Zabish who was still no more than a limp rag doll. A bewildered Berhanu was following Hahn carefully, not wanting to lose his last remaining child.

Dartey did not regret this search even though he recognized it as being neurotic and self serving. They had bypassed hundreds of dying people and selected two individuals to comfort themselves and to prove to themselves that "something was being done". He regarded it as a way of disassociating themselves from the whole lamentable human mistake that was famine.

With the rediscovery of Berhanu and Zabish Hahn stopped muttering, "This is a hell-hole." As they drove out of the camp he appeared more relaxed and less breathless. Some desperate mothers rushed towards the car and placed their babies in its path. The driver neatly avoided them and was grateful that this time his passengers did not ask him to stop.

Dear Lili,

I have a terrible hangover. I have led a sheltered life. Last night was my first night at a first night in the West End theatre.

In a dim haze I can remember that you were absolutely first rate. I must have told you that.

I am going to sit and contemplate for a while and then write a more coherent letter.

Love,
Henry

Dear Henry,

I feel obliged to place on record the occurrences of the first night as it seems to be such a blank to you.

At least half a dozen people have told me that there was only one star and one sensation of the evening. It was Henry Smith. Henry Smith wearing a frilly pink shirt, dark pink velvet bow tie, and a shiny black suit. Henry Smith, having dispatched his wheelchair, speeding at an incredible rate of knots to his seat in the centre of the stalls like a manic clockwork mouse, and then being the first to the bar in the interval having passed through the throngs of stunned onlookers like Moses through the Red Sea. Henry Smith being bought a drink by everyone at the bar, inundated with wine, champagne and brandy and then fairly twinkling at the party afterwards, in fact *the* sensation of the evening. If only half that drama had been happening on the stage. I won't be at all surprised if Henry Smith is included in reviews of the play.

Unlike you, the parents were models of decorum. Although I did hear our mother telling Ian that the theatre was in our family blood and that she always knew I would be a star. And she said that without blushing which, I suppose, proves that she's a very good actress indeed.

Anyway, I'm relieved that it's over. Now we have to get on with the business of doing it every night. My dance, which seemed so astounding to me months ago in the farther reaches of Clapham, has now become my daily bread and butter. I'm already appalled at the idea of having to do this play eight times a week. I've pinned up a chart on the dressing room wall and I'm marking off the days till my six months are up.

What diabolic mind concocted this malevolent form of

torture, making actors do and say the same thing night after night? It's like working on an assembly line manufacturing Ford Cortinas, only instead of fitting the same door panel time after time it's the same words.

You have probably forgotten our rather inebriated conversation about Mr Dartey. You were advising me to go to Africa and seek him out as it was a *great passion*. You were quite insistent and offered to come with me. I think you just want an excuse to go abroad. I really don't know why we are still talking about him. It's always you that starts these conversations now. I think you miss Mr Dartey.

Love,
Lili

P.S. The reviews are coming in slowly, *very* slowly. The critics didn't exactly kill themselves to speed their reviews into the paper. Our first night was staged forty-five minutes earlier than usual, presumably so they could all rush home and write their reviews before midnight; not one has availed himself of this great opportunity. If we had tried to emulate the first night parties at Sardi's in New York and waited to read the first reviews, we would have had a long and extremely boring party. Can you imagine Henry, you'd still be at it knocking back those brandy alexanders!

An hour after leaving Tekl El Bab, Hahn and Dartey drove into Kassala which with its fully green landscape and underground river, its brick and mud houses daubed with bright splashes of yellow and pink, seemed almost frivolous in comparison to the grim scenes they had just left. Berhanu stared in disbelief at a stall vendor pouring out glasses of cold guava juice, while Zabish lay frighteningly still on the car seat beside him. It was a cruel joke that this lush oasis of citrus and mango groves, date palms and vegetable plots was only an hour's drive from thousands of starving people.

Kassala, always a base for the various aid organizations, was now simply awash with relief workers of every description. DAF was well represented and its vehicles stamped with the familiar bold blue initials were all over town.

Hahn instructed the driver to go straight to the DAF compound. As his daughter was carried into the clinic, Berhanu stepped out stiffly and followed with some difficulty, but did not once let the child out of his sight. Zabish, who showed no visible signs of life, was examined by an Italian paediatrician. It appeared that apart from being badly dehydrated and starved, she had bronchial pneumonia. The paediatrician thought that it might be too late to save Zabish but she would do everything she could.

Berhanu listened uncomprehendingly to discussions on the case that were carried out in a variety of European languages. He seemed to be standing upright only by a fierce act of will, but this enabled him to follow his daughter to the children's ward and remain resolutely by her bedside. Hahn was reluctant to leave the ward and had to be urged away by Dartey.

The famine was beginning to take its emotional toll on Hahn and he appeared momentarily stripped of any defences. It seemed to Dartey that there were two Hahns, one the dispassionate businessman who was convinced that DAF should be run as efficiently as his kitchen appliance factory in Norwich and who believed in everyone toeing the DAF line and being a good company man. The other Hahn, the one who had come to Africa, was sensitive and sentimental and could not cope with all the suffering. Dartey felt that if he had brought his other self with him and left the soft sentimental one to administer the London office, it might have had a beneficent effect all round and might prove a rule of thumb for everyone in the aid business.

Dartey and Hahn booked two extremely inexpensive rooms at the austere Bashair Hotel. The former lay on his bed and thanked God for the opportunity to be alone, the latter spent a fortune on the telephone to his wife who had flown to Florida and thereby compounded his distress.

Later that afternoon they met a group of DAF workers at the hotel and discussed ways of cutting through the red tape that was keeping several hundred tons of grain in Port Sudan.

No great conclusions were reached. The only small hope lay in Hahn and Dartey buttonholing the right officials when they reached Khartoum the next day.

After the others had gone, Hahn half begged and half ordered Dartey to stay and celebrate the New Year which was not due for another five days. Another pitiful case of mistiming, Dartey thought.

Outside the sun dropped rapidly behind the enormous granite jebels, whose distinctive outline towered over Kassala and protected it from the omnipresence of the desert beyond. Hahn took a bottle of Scotch from his suitcase and searched for glasses, while regretting that Christmas had slipped through their fingers.

"Purely medicinal." He handed Dartey a large dose. Then falling back on to his bed he announced, "I'm going to hold a Miss DAF contest in absentia."

"What for?"

"What for!" Hahn stared at Dartey as though he were a particularly troublesome pupil in an unruly class.

Hahn launched into a discourse on the relative merits of all the female employees of DAF in the Sahel: he imagined them, despite their uncoiffured hair and tired faces, parading in swimsuits and high heels around the room. His ability to mentally reconstruct the physical attributes of every DAF woman stationed from Mauritania to the Sudan astonished Dartey and gave evidence of a mental prowess not exhibited before. The winner was announced after half an hour of deep reflection: she was an Australian nutritionist in Timbuktu. The Italian paediatrician they had met earlier in the day was a runner up.

After this effort Hahn became quite inebriated and stood on the bed and quoted Genesis chapter one, verse twenty-seven. According to him, "Male and female created he them" indicated that mankind was created as a combination of both sexes. He said that cohabitation with his wife had forced him into a male role and her into a female role. In his opinion they would be individually more complete if they were to live apart.

Dartey, who was himself quietly and unnoticeably drunk,

asked how this sort of logic could come from one who had just staged the Miss DAF contest. But he received no answer. Hahn had slumped wordless into a chair.

The following morning the two men, chastened and red-eyed, visited the clinic in the DAF compound. One doctor remarked that Hahn's face looked like a monkey's arse.

The frail Zabish appeared, if possible, smaller and thinner as she lay very still, submerged under tubes and drips. Berhanu, silent and indomitable as ever, stared at them curiously and made the indulgences of the night before seem even more farcical.

On the plane to Khartoum Dartey looked down at the miles of parched brown earth and found in them something akin to that silent stare, something accusatory.

The ebullient, verbose Hahn was now wordless and looked ready to have another bout of diarrhoea.

For the first time in two days Dartey thought of the girl, Lili Smith, and was relieved to discover he had gone so long without her. If he had made this much progress he could make more.

Dear Lili,

How can you be bored already? The play only opened last Tuesday. Although I must say I did mention to our mother that you were getting bored and she said, "Well she would, wouldn't she? It's been almost a week now."

I'm sure you must have read all the reviews by now. I have been collecting them. I will use them in the book and devote a whole chapter to the peculiar variety of human opinions. It's amazing to me that a group of people can sit in an auditorium, watch exactly the same thing and arrive at such wildly different conclusions. It makes me wonder what other people see when I see pink or orange. It makes me wonder how I can discuss anything with anyone if there is no common experience to draw on.

And finally, if the reviews are all so different, why bother with them in the first place because all the readers will think differently too? I'm a newcomer to reviews, having only read yours. Perhaps sometimes they all agree on something. If so, it is purely by chance, as when everything falls into place in a fruit machine.

I think I've read them all, dailies, Sundays and weeklies. Somewhere in this cauldron of opinions are a few truths (according to me). I believe actors traditionally nurture the insults and forget the flattery. Why not be a first and do the reverse! Knowing your morbid tendencies I know you won't but I hang it up there, a perverse possibility for your examination.

What do you think of these priceless excerpts I've chosen to appear in the book?

The Guardian: The cadences of the lines echo uncannily the early works of Pinter and one is reminded of the Theatre of the Absurd, particularly of *The Bald Prima Donna*. It is a curiously evocative work and not what it seems at first glance.

The Times: The play seems to have aspirations to be an existential French movie with interminable scenes and suffocatingly boring dialogue interspersed with irrelevant songs and dances. I pitied the poor actors burdened with such complete balderdash. The production seemed intent on accentuating the tedium and weaknesses of the work of a novice writer.

Daily Telegraph: David McNair conveys excellently the contrast between the devoted husband and betrayed and suicidal lover. He gives a magnificent display of depth and passion rarely seen on the London stage.

Spectator: Ian Harding can be congratulated for catching the exact tone of this unusual piece.

Time Out: David McNair provides a display of raw energy which is almost embarrassing in its intensity.

Observer: Lili Smith seems uncomfortable and amateurish in the leading role and does not have the figure for cavorting naked around the stage to bowdlerized Bach.

Financial Times: David McNair strived too hard for theatricality and seemed miscast as the ill-fated husband.

Daily Mail: Lili Smith is the West End's new dancing sensation. She reveals all in a dramatic and sexy dance that should keep this play running for a long time.

Sunday Times: Single handedly Lili Smith saves a mediocre play and provides it with one of the most compelling musical moments I've seen in years.

The Standard: Eleanor Bright's first play is a strange mishmash of styles and has no real content. It is a collection of scenes backed by early seventies Euro-pop. It's not a musical, not a comedy, and not a serious play. It left me confused and wishing I was home watching *Dynasty*.

So there you are. All my favourite bits. If you think I've left anything really worthy out, let me know.

Love,
Henry

Dear Henry,

I am speechless with rage over the reviews. It only proves to me that there are a lot of (don't put this in the book) mentally deficient blind and deaf people writing reviews for the British press.

My chief bone of contention is David McNair. I've been watching him for weeks thinking that he's a star so he must know what he's doing even if he isn't half as good as Brian in the part. I thought that his mugging and odd vocal stresses were exercises to approach the role. But I've discovered to my horror that, no that was it, that was his performance! He's the kind of actor who dramatizes each word and makes nonsense of the entire speech. If he comes across the word "boat" he makes little wavy motions with his hands.

Like sneezing or hiccupping this sort of thing gets attention and while he has it, he creates little pools of meaninglessness in Eleanor's poor battered play.

Then to see those comments about his performance! All I can say is that they have sat through so many plays that their brains have locked or cemented, or whatever over-worked brains do. Even the one criticism of David merely said that "he strived too hard for theatricality and seemed miscast". Why couldn't someone say that "David McNair mugged and cavorted like an astronaut with a wasp in his suit and did not have the faintest idea what he was doing. His entire performance screamed, Me, Me, Me!"

The critics may be happy to know that encouraged by their comments David is doing twice as much of what he did before, more grimaces, contortions, squeaks and groans.

As for me I'm marking off the days and looking forward to an early retirement. Your book may be shorter than expected.

Love,
Lili

P.S. Did you see today's *Guardian*? There is a photograph of a troubled and concerned Ian alongside an interview where he states that the play is about the corruption of British upper class society and the rape of the innocence of the working classes. And I bet he said it with a straight face. All I will say is that the rape of innocence and corruption behind the scenes was far more intense and dramatic then anything on the stage, but like the play it had repetitive dialogue and lacked structure.

P.P.S. I dreamed about Mr Dartey last night. I blame it on the Hollandaise sauce I was persuaded to eat in a lethal French restaurant. I hate going out to dinner after the theatre.

Now they were in Ethiopia following in a path already trodden by politicians, film stars and church leaders, a celebrity circus that had flashed names like Alamata, Mekele, Korem and Kobo around the world.

Just like those who had blazed the trail before them, they were humble witnesses to the superhuman efforts of the relief workers who were struggling under impossible conditions. The workers were not only fighting the sickness of others but a variety of ailments they had succumbed to themselves. One nurse continued to work long hours with a drip attached to her arm and looked hardly better than those she was helping. Hahn could not simply stand by and trailed after her like a faithful dog trying to help with vaccinations and the feeding of children who were unable to eat. "Mmm! Good!" he would say like someone in a television commercial to children who would smile and then vomit.

Dartey noted that everywhere they went Hahn's effusive goodwill was appreciated by refugee and relief worker alike, even if his bumbling attempts to help usually resulted in more rather than less work for others.

On January 21st they reached Addis Ababa and found the Hilton Hotel bustling with journalists comparing notes about the famine. Hahn was enormously relieved by the sense of occasion there and flitted around like a debutante at her first ball.

Apart from seeing at a distance a busload of journalists pursuing a visiting politician, they had met very few representatives of the media in their long trek across the Sahel. They had not realized until then that they were all assembled in the Addis Ababa Hilton. Even Dartey's jaundiced eye was pleased at the sight of what seemed like well fed visitors from another planet. Their presence was stirring: they were not worn down by the situation and they brought a fresh view.

Having deposited Hahn at the Hilton, Dartey was on his way out when he was stopped by a man carrying a large bag of photographic equipment, a tall, smiling man with hair like Hahn's, blond streaks across a balding crown. He told Dartey that he was a Norwegian journalist who had arrived that morning from Kassala. A woman doctor working in the DAF compound there had asked him to give Dartey a Polaroid photograph if by any chance their paths should cross. He had recognized Dartey immediately from her description "tall, dark, and hostile".

The Norwegian handed over a photograph which was streaked with white paste: he apologized for this, explaining that it had been packed alongside a leaking tube of toothpaste. The photograph showed a woman leaning over a child in a hospital bed. The woman was laughing because the child's fingers were grasped firmly round a strand of her hair and trapping her in a bent position. The child's eyes were remarkably alert like those of someone who was grateful to have awakened from a bad dream. The child was Zabish, photographed here with the attractive Italian paediatrician. It was just over two weeks since they had left her in Kassala.

Dartey thanked the Norwegian with extreme haste and grabbed the photograph: he raced across the lobby to Hahn, who upon seeing it did a little jig and received a few odd stares. Zabish had not died and would continue to live judging from her improved appearance in the photo. She was not exactly plump and robust but she would live and for the two tired men it was a small life saved, a large victory.

It was these victories that sustained all the workers they had met and somehow prevented them from being submerged in the far more numerous defeats. So many mothers weeping over so many children, so many small bodies placed in shallow graves, these were black pictures that required some balancing, some solace.

Zabish had been selected to live, a process that Dartey had witnessed far too often. It was an invidious power, this power of life and death that he had seen wielded by unhappy doctors as they tested the thickness of an arm and selected who should be saved and who should be left to struggle against impossible odds. He hoped never to see it again, but it was a faint hope.

On examining the Polaroid photograph Dartey noticed Berhanu almost out of frame, his shoulders and half his face visible, standing in his steady vigil by the bedside. For some time he studied the droop of the shoulders, the set of the face, looking for clues to his disposition and his state of health. He realized that he was now fully committed to the welfare of Berhanu and Zabish: he had opened himself up to them because he could not open himself to everyone. He shared them with Hahn. Here was a small, manageable tragedy; he would be effective and retain a small sense of dominion in the middle of an enormous tide of suffering and death.

Dear Lili,

I came up to London yesterday for an interview at an office near Goodge Street station. I won't bother to tell you anything about the substance of the interview except to say that it was quite farcical, even to the point of everyone talking as though I wasn't there. "He doesn't understand that . . ." "He couldn't cope with the . . ." "It's a shame he's come all this way." All spoken over my head as though my wheelchair was encased in a soundproofed box and I couldn't hear a word. When they did address me it was loudly and slowly to enable me to read their lips through the window in the soundproofed box.

Anyway I have grown beyond fits of temper on these occasions. Or let's say, I'm working on getting beyond it. I whizzed up the Tottenham Court Road and looked around to see if I could find the place where you used to rehearse, but had no luck. Then I caught the Central Line to Notting Hill Gate, presuming, my dear sister, to visit you but you weren't in.

So, for want of anything to do, I went down to Ladbroke Grove and re-examined the DAF U.K. headquarters in the mews by the Metropolitan railway line. I sat for a while watching people go in and out the main door. I began to see that it comprises three houses joined together, converted into one large office building but in no way modernized or beautified. Old stables used for years as garages or workshops are now lumped ungraciously together.

In the interests of research for the Dartey section of the book I felt obliged to go in . There were no steps so it was easy to wheel into the reception area where I waited for ages completely ignored.

It's a really dreggy old dump with some extremely pretty girls wandering about. Mr. Dartey need not have wasted his time on you: the DAF building is a real source! No one questioned my presence. Everyone seemed to think I belonged to someone else and they were all very polite and remote. So I just sat there for awhile and became part of the scenery.

It occurred to me while I was sitting there that people in wheelchairs fall into a very exclusive category. They are largely ignored and avoided. I could hire myself out for espionage work or the more difficult type of robbery. I would place the secret microfilms or purloined articles under the seat of my wheelchair and no one would stop me because they would be fearful of getting into a conversation.

I finally managed to block the pathway of one of the scurrying females, a devastatingly attractive girl with dark curly hair, and told her that I approved of the shabbiness of the facilities because it proved to the world that DAF U.K. was not wasting funds on its own comfort and I also told her that a close relative had worked for Mr Dartey. The latter proved to be most effective. I was immediately taken to meet Bert Hahn's assistant in a cold damp room at the back.

The assistant is the only really ugly woman in the building but very friendly and overworked. The phone kept ringing. But in between calls I managed to tell her that I would like to know what Mr Dartey was doing. She showed me a file of reports sent back by Mr Dartey which I thought was a tremendous coup. So I can give you profuse details about their tour across the Sahel, if you're interested.

I think I could get myself a job at DAF if I played my cards right because they need help in this current crisis. They have been inundated with letters and contributions. The famine can't last much longer with this kind of help pouring in. But they do need workers. I think I might go and hang out there again as it only takes me about an hour and a half to get there from home.

Love from
Henry

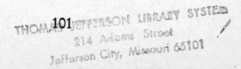

Dear Henry,

Please make no further references to Mr Dartey. I would hardly call information about him a "tremendous coup". Would you stop dredging up the past.

In the biographies of famous stars chapters are not devoted to former employers, especially one like Mr Dartey who has nothing to recommend him except his rather lavish appearance.

Your book is in danger of becoming an unauthorized biography if you do not accede to the star's wishes.

Love,
Lili

Dear Lili,

The trouble with most stars' biographies is that they become monotonous. Early struggles then success, with a series of titles and dates interspersed with a few divorces and breakdowns.

Mr Dartey was, after all, an integral part of your life for a good part of 1984, and you were quite an EVENT for him. Writing about him enables me to include some interesting information about his work for DAF.

In the cause of bringing added texture to the book I've been to the library and done a little research on Ethiopia and discovered that thirty years ago the plateaux in northern Ethiopia were abundant with grain and vegetables. The land was flowing with milk, so much so that the women washed their clothes in a mixture of water and milk, and were able to follow the traditional custom of rubbing butter over their skin as a sort of cosmetic.

As the population increased they cut down trees and did not replace them. They overgrazed the land and knew nothing about fertilizing and rotating crops. Now even if the rains come they will still need assistance as they have eaten their seeds and the oxen are either dead or too weak to plough.

I found this extremely interesting because in one of his reports Mr Dartey gives a completely different reason for the famine. He writes that the 1973 famine was exacerbated by the feudal regime of Haile Selassie but that the new Marxist regime brought no improvement. For generations Ethiopian village life was finely balanced on a system of sharing in which each man would co-operate with another. One farmer would lend his donkey to another, in return he would be loaned clay pots for the storage of grain, and so on. All the villagers were individually responsible for their possessions and animals yet they were shared. And in times of drought they shared the stored grain.

Then with the new Marxist regime came the collectivization of the villages where no one owned anything. Animals that were proudly looked after before became neglected without a personal owner. The stored grain was taken by the government to feed the army and to be used for the government's own political reasons and when the drought came there were no reserves and the people starved.

I suppose an old lefty like Mr Dartey must be criticizing here the incorrect application of Marxist principles because what villages had going before was a pure and primitive Marxism.

Anyway, Lili, don't flap about my Mr Dartey chapter (perhaps not even a chapter just a few well-researched paragraphs). Famous people have to face up to the fact that the public is interested in every facet of their lives. At least I write with taste and discretion. You have to prepare yourself for the invasion of mawkish, sensationalizing, entirely unsympathetic writers. One of the prices of fame.

Love,
Henry

Dear Henry,

If you want to write about the breaking up of Ethiopian village life, please go ahead. But don't squeeze it into my biography. You seem to forget that I spent six months typing up all that sort of stuff for old granite-faced Dartey and I would consider it a gross injustice to have to be reminded of it every time I opened up the story of my life.

You do not know everything. You have had a remarkably short life and little experience so far. You are only twenty-two. Stop pontificating about my career and keep in your place. You are just my little brother, don't forget.

Lili

Dear Lili,

Keep your hair on. I may be only twenty-two, but don't forget that Buddy Holly had accomplished more than almost anyone you care to mention when he died at twenty-two.

Your loving brother
Henry

After going through Customs at Heathrow airport Dartey and Hahn did not stop to wish each other goodbye. Hahn rushed off to look for his wife who was waiting somewhere with a chauffeur and Dartey carried his small case and typewriter down to the Piccadilly Line.

Sitting on the train observing the alien blank faces of his fellow passengers, Dartey realised that he was back in London and he was free of the girl. All that silliness was over. He would not haunt her restaurant, she would not haunt his thoughts, he would get on with his life.

Yesterday, at Hahn's request, he had sat by the pool of the

Norfolk Hotel in Nairobi and watched bronzed men in safari shirts and khaki shorts yelling at the waiters. He did not listen while Hahn talked about his wife, instead he studied Hahn's face, which was painfully red and scabrous from an excess of sun, a face that had developed a few interesting concavities in its once soft, bulbous surface.

"Funny things women," Hahn said.

"Yes, absolutely."

"Are you married Dartey?" He had asked this question many times as though displeased with the original reply and wishing to get a different one.

"No, are you?"

"Yes to my wife, I was just talking about her."

"Oh, right, of course your wife."

Along with the director of DAF U.K. Dartey directed a pair of tired squinting eyes towards a young woman in a red silk dress who wafted up and down as she waited for someone who never came. The shimmering fabric of her dress caught the light and gave out a red glow like an ignominious invitation. It reminded Dartey of the shiny orange sofa on which he had abused the girl.

Was it abuse? It wasn't rape and it wasn't seduction. A milder term, perhaps, was "taken advantage". He was relieved to feel that he had no more desire to take advantage of her.

His flat in Little Venice was still pleasingly uncluttered. He liked its lack of furniture and made a mental note that the orange sofa would go the following morning. If no one would take it he would hack it into little pieces and put it in the dustbin.

The cleaner had piled his mail on his desk and consumed all the tea and coffee. Things were back to normal. His anger was bubbling away at a level he could handle. He was home and he was himself again.

Part Three

Dear Henry,

Last night was a disaster. In the face of an unexpected incident I behaved like a simpering half-wit. Aren't leading actresses supposed to have a little social aplomb? I don't think that I ever will now, I'm too old to change.

It happened at one of those charity jobs I keep doing. It's amazing how much one gets involved in this sort of work as a minor "name" and how quickly one goes from being a charity case to a worker for it. This time it was a ball in a stately home somewhere in Suffolk, whereabouts in Suffolk I know not, as I was delivered there post-haste as a last minute replacement for the midnight cabaret. I had to leap into a car that was waiting at the stage door on Saturday night and was instructed to learn my song and dance in the car!

Suffolk is a dark obscure place at night and I had no idea where we were going, though I did notice that we drove through a distinctive village market place just before we arrived. The driver told me that the old timber framed houses in this part of the village were built by Flemish weavers and wool merchants in the 14th and 15th centuries; but I was not in the mood for appreciating the wonders of medieval architecture as I was listening to tape recorded instructions. "Arms outstretched and kick and turn. Turn and kick . . . etc., etc."

We went up a long driveway to a large old country residence past the Rolls and Jaguars and round to the kitchen door at the back. I was hustled into a pantry by an hysterical wardrobe lady and director, who were gibbering with horror at my late arrival. I was garbed in a much fatter actress's sequined costume which slipped too low and fell open too far. I tried to clutch it in place as I rehearsed the steps around the kitchen table, then ten minutes later I was pushed out on to the stage in the ballroom where I danced one step behind two other actresses who knew what they were doing. We sang the song I'd learned in the car and somehow I managed to waffle through it. For this the audience had paid a great deal of money and with the fortunate distortion of perception given by champagne, they applauded loudly.

Afterwards I paused to admire the taffeta and satin haute couture gowns and the intimidating supply of diamonds dangling everywhere, then I escaped and went on a tour of the house or rather one 18th century wing. I climbed up to the old servants' quarters at the top which were as tiny and cramped as a rabbit warren, each bed or bunk being merely partitioned with no door, therefore no privacy. Then I went down the back stairs to the stables, which were far more expansive than the servant's quarters.

I stood there shivering in the fat actress's sequined gown which gaped open and exposed me to cold shafts of air and I thought about the life of an 18th century horse which must have been more comfortable than a servant's life.

From the stables I could see across a mossy courtyard into the ballroom where the dancers were moving about like sparkling puppets. Their laughter and the music were muffled behind thick oak doors and closed windows, but I could hear the faint sound of the orchestra playing a quadrille. Past the ballroom the courtyard led out to a mass of black-green grass which sloped down to a lake. There was a moon, of course: this was a fat moon which reminded me of the actress whose dress I was wearing. It threw a soft, diaphanous light on to the lake and the willow trees around it. And there were stars, hundreds of them, clearer and sharper than they are in London.

Then, feeling I'm sure that this was a suitably romantic setting, along came Mr Dartey.

I found out later that his presence was not all that surprising as the ball had been given to raise money for the African famine and he had given a speech just before I arrived. I think I was told what the charity was but it hadn't really registered in all the panic about the performance. So when he appeared around the side of the stables he seemed like an apparition coming out of the shadows.

We were both more than surprised, thunder-struck is perhaps the word. On reflection I realize that he must have seen me in the cabaret and was sneaking round the backway to escape. He looked as though the last person he wanted to see was me.

For a few seconds he stood in the shadows obviously contemplating a quick retreat, then he came forward and said, "Good evening." He was very formal. In the half light I could see that his face was a lot more calm and perceptive than I remembered it. He seemed to see what I was and to dismiss it, which had the effect of making me want to prove that he was mistaken.

But I did not prove anything. I giggled. It was two in the morning. I had done a matinee and an evening performance and then that nerve-wracking cabaret appearance. I was not mentally ready for Mr Dartey. I think that the perfect moon, the willow tree, the music, the full quota of stars etc. and this perfect creature coming round the corner, looming dark and magnificent—it was all too much for me.

My giggling seemed to confirm what Mr Dartey had already assumed about me and seemed to be yet another way of rejecting him. He began to look past me checking on his way of escape. Then he did escape and walked past me quickly. I said, "Sorry" hurriedly, which is all I ever seem to say to him. "Don't be," he said and kept on walking.

Then I felt wretched because I had undermined a dramatic encounter, our first meeting in four months. But there was nothing I could do, he disappeared around the corner and a minute or so later I heard a car going down the drive.

After that I went inside and looked at the books in the library. (They had a good selection of books on archery, Henry, some of them quite ancient, you would have loved them.) Then I waited until I could find someone to drive me back to London. I suppose I should have danced the night away but instead I sat and brooded. I had found Mr Dartey's calmness extremely disturbing and was trying to think what I had done to make him so calm.

Tomorrow is my one hundredth performance of this, to be kind, flawed play. And that's not including all the nights at *The Princess Louise*. The repetition is killing me. Perhaps if I were doing Shakespeare I would be so busy trying to understand what I was saying that I wouldn't notice the eight performances a week and I wouldn't be marking off the days like a convict serving twenty years. But this is not Shakespeare, it's Eleanor Bright and the constant repetition is playing some strange tricks on my mind. When I say one line, I hold the previous line and the next line in my head and sometimes when I pause to think I don't know which one of the three lines I have said.

This kind of thinking can cause paralysis. Automatic pilot works better. There's a lot of it going on in this production. I think some actors do their laundry lists or plan menus while they are on stage: that's why people who see a play after it has been running several months are not getting the play, they are getting laundry lists and menus.

David McNair suffers no torment however. He is another kind of actor. His mind does not play tricks on him because there was no mind there in the first place. He was made for long runs.

The run of this play is going to outlast my contract. The only way I can get out before my contract expires is by becoming pregnant or insane. The latter seems quite a possibility. Right now the house is reasonably full every night. We get a lot of Japanese businessmen and sheiks who sit like ghosts in the stalls, brought there, I presume, by reports of a titillating dance; and then there are the coach parties who come in from all over the place. The play has become a monument people visit when they are in London.

Ian is even having discussions about taking the play to New York, which just goes to show that I know nothing about the minds of the populace and their tastes, and that Ian knows everything. Do I want to live in such a world?

The parents have been to see the play five times in three

months. They meet me at the stage door with shining eyes and rosy glows on their cheeks. And that at the moment seems to be what it's all about—all those years of discipline and deprivation have amounted to—cheering up the parents.

Love,
Lili

The meeting with Lili Smith, a meeting Dartey knew would happen eventually, was held somewhere in an obscure region of his mind. It was not held up for examination. The pain and discomfort associated with her had subsided and would remain so.

The dance in Suffolk was not a personal choice of his, in fact one of the reasons he had spent fifteen years in Africa was to avoid things like that dance. Such occasions were uphill all the way for him. He had gone to the dance in an official capacity to make a speech. The speech was easy. But the effort to make light conversation afterwards was taxing. He could not chat. His mind froze and ideas had to be dredged up with a superhuman effort that exhausted him.

Only the speech flowed, which was fortunate as he was currently required to give four or five speeches a week.

"You really are a stupid arse, Dartey, the way you pontificate all over the place," Hahn had said the day before the dance.

He meant that Dartey should devote more of his speech to raising money for DAF and less to the analysis of Africa's problems which, according to Hahn, turned people off.

Dartey did in fact try to keep his speeches light especially when confronted with fidgety girls in strapless dresses and their blank-faced escorts.

Personally he battled with the thought that the problems of Africa were beyond the capacities of any government or agency, let alone a charity ball, to meet. So far, it was true, that continent had been drowned in a sea of good and not so good intentions, but he had to believe that this could change. He had to believe it and he would. He had no other alternative. This belief, however, had its bad days.

He had framed one report and hung it on the wall in Hahn's office. The report stated that in one year three hundred and sixty-two international missions visited a single African country to plan assistance projects. Officials in charge had no time for anything except meeting the visiting foreigners. The country was kept in a retrogressive limbo for an entire year; or perhaps longer, as Dartey pointed out to Hahn, because those kinds of visitations continue to multiply themselves and become a way of life for all concerned.

Hahn in his turn sent Dartey a framed picture of a naked woman. A packet of seeds in a small plastic bag was taped as a sort of a fig leaf on to the woman's body. These seeds, according to Hahn, were samples of the new high yield drought-resistant sorghum which could bring about a green revolution in Africa and produce the great economic change that every one dreamed of.

Hahn received by return a note which said, "We'll see."

The picture was still lying by the front door where he had left it when Dartey arrived home from the dance in Suffolk just before dawn. He fell into bed and awoke several hours later to find bright sunshine and shadows dappling his bed. His dress shirt was hanging over a lamp and his jacket and trousers were crumpled in a heap on the floor. He picked the suit up and put it on a hanger in an effort to remove the creases. He was to wear it again that evening at a formal dinner at his mother's house.

Today was the much-discussed, much-heralded last day of Gabrielle's long tour of duty with Catherine Dartey. For this special day the mistress had compiled the longest most complex menu for her retiring cook to present to as many guests as could squeeze round her dining room table. She was using up the last of Gabrielle. Dartey was not looking forward to it.

The awkward meeting with Lili Smith had, by the morning, resolved itself into a slight indigestive feeling. He could live with that. Images flashed in his mind, unasked for and unheralded. She had looked almost unearthly standing there in a sort of gossamer, sparkly dress that barely covered her, like something out of *A Midsummer Night's Dream*.

But she was a mere mortal and had proved so many times. The images were instantly dismissed. He had purged himself of her and needed no further reminders. That is why her phone call came as an assault and made him angrier than he thought possible.

The time of the call recorded on his bedside digital clock was eleven forty-five a.m. He knew that it was her before she spoke: he could feel her presence. That was the first thing that made him angry. It was an invasion, an act of will on her part.

"Hello, this is . . ." She paused apologetically, ". . . Lili Smith."

He also paused a long time before he said, "Yes." He found the anger made breathing difficult.

"Yes it is I'm afraid."

"What do you want?"

"I'm sorry about the way things have turned out. I was wondering if we could meet." She sounded nervous or she was giving a performance of nervousness.

"What for?"

"What for. . . ? Just a meeting really."

"I don't think that's a good idea."

"No I didn't think you would." She sighed.

There was a long pause.

Then she spoke again. "I'd like to say sorry then."

"You've said that."

"I know." She sighed again.

"Is that it?"

"Yes."

"Goodbye then."

"Goodbye."

He put the phone down. He could detect subterfuge in a tone or a look, sometimes before it had become a conscious thought. He could smell it. He did not like manipulative women. He had always avoided them.

The phone rang again. He let it ring for some time before he picked up the receiver. It was his mother complaining bitterly about Gabrielle who was refusing to cook the items on the menu which she considered redundant. She also refused to wear any kind of uniform for her last performance.

Dartey said very little. Catherine merely needed to let off some steam. The relationship between his mother and Gabrielle was wrapped in mystery and depended on antagonism to give it buoyancy. He knew better than to interfere.

When he arrived at his mother's house later that evening dressed in a crumpled suit and rather sweaty dress shirt he walked quickly and silently through the assembled guests and took refuge in the garden. As if on cue, all the guests flooded out after him.

It was an unusually warm evening for the end of March. Some of the ladies were wearing flimsy mid-summer dresses and moving like phosphorescent butterflies among the flowers in the garden. Dartey backed up until he was against the far wall of the small garden. He observed the women with their painted faces and jewellery, their carefully chosen, artfully angled clothes that plunged and zig-zagged. It seemed ridiculous to him that this assemblage of flesh and artifice should have such power over men. A woman could look at a man in a certain way and he would follow her anywhere. With the stricture of that power, friendship with such individuals seemed impossible.

Dartey examined his tricky escapes from emotionally needy women and the series of carefree arrangements with their more obliging and undemanding sisters that he'd had in the past. Had there been any friendship involved? On reflection they seemed like business deals, cool and unemotional. They had suited the needs of the moment exactly. And the recent months of turmoil over Lili Smith only proved how sensible the previous arrangements had been. He had never been friends with a woman.

He heard his mother's voice ordering the guests into the dining room and all those who flooded out, flooded in again. Alone in the dusk he observed the flowers which grew alongside the path. The very English spring flowers with their delicate misty colours deepened and darkened under his intense observation until they became stunning pink and red bougainvillaea. He had sat and stared at those great flashes of mesmerizing colour while on a brief visit to a ranch outside Nairobi. It was an evening of escape from Hahn. He was able to sit in silence and watch the stars which were close enough to touch. For a while the quiet patience of Africa, so much a part of the people, seemed to rise from the soil and give him a momentary peace.

But now there was no peace. His mother was calling him in a voice of high-pitched irritation. They were all seated and waiting and had been for some time. Dartey went inside briskly.

Mrs Dartey had employed two maids in black dresses and white aprons to serve the dinner. She watched them critically, but could find no fault. All was running smoothly until Gabrielle appeared from the kitchen. She was wearing a shabby, flowered print dress which was not helped by her broad Teutonic shoulders and stout legs, and a tea towel covered in gravy stains tied around her waist. Catherine Dartey flinched at the sight of her.

She set down a dish on the table in front of her mistress and rubbed her back as she straightened, letting out a small groan. In her heavy German accent she said, "You should provide me with more help in the kitchen. Don't just spend the money where it shows." Then she turned and trudged towards the kitchen still rubbing her back.

"Gabrielle," said Catherine loudly enough for Gabrielle and all the guests to hear, "voted for Hitler in 1932. She thought he was quite amazing."

Gabrielle's hand momentarily stopped rubbing her back but she continued her forward motion, threw the kitchen door open and slammed it behind her.

It seemed, thought Dartey, that women could be as deadly to each other as they were to the opposite sex.

Henry waited for over an hour in the entrance hall. The lady in the ticket office provided a chair because she had been offended by the sight of him on the floor "like a beggar". The long wait was his own choice. He had arrived early to honour the special

117

occasion, Lili's first visit home in five months. A celebratory pot of tea was being prepared in the flat upstairs and the word had been telegraphed to the various corners of the Berkeley Road Baths that Lili was coming.

She arrived in a dark mood and stared bitterly at her brother. He'd had his hair cut very short like stubbly corn and was expecting her to notice but she merely said, "I did what you told me. It was a disaster."

Henry sat immobile holding his head at an angle so that she would get the full shock effect of the jagged hair. "Did what?" he asked.

"I phoned him. You are a bloody idiot Henry." She stood over her brother, her shoulders drooping, a picture of mortification and regret.

"What did he say?"

"Basically, fuck off. I don't know why I listened to you. I should have dropped the whole thing. That was my instinct."

The misery in his sister's face made him realize that it would be some time before his hairstyle received any attention. He dropped his head. The two became silent islands amid the crowding Saturday morning swimmers.

Henry broke the silence and spoke tentatively. "I didn't tell you to phone him."

"Henry you did!"

"When?"

"Oh I don't know, two or three months ago."

"He wasn't in the country then."

"Oh Henry!"

"And anyway you wouldn't follow my instructions. You've always been so dead against having anything to do with him."

"Because he's a cardboard cutout, that's why. There's nothing to him except what you see."

"Lili, be serious, you know I couldn't make you do anything you didn't want to do."

Lili did not answer. She stood in silence and chewed her lip as she used to when she was a small child and stood over Henry's cot watching the baby whose legs didn't move.

"Oh it doesn't matter." She gave his foot the customary

kick indicating that he should move off. "I like the neo-punk hair."

Henry smiled and dropped to the floor. He slithered towards the stairs and paused for thought thus entangling himself in the legs of two prospective swimmers. He looked up at Lili. "Please disregard anything I've said on the subject of Mr Dartey, or anything I might say. I think we should both avoid mentioning him in future."

"That's what I've wanted all along," Lili cried out in a shrill voice which caused several members of the public to turn and watch her. They observed as Lili kicked her brother's foot and hustled him up the stairs.

They went on up to the first floor flat and enjoyed a serene cup of tea with their parents. Shirley and Roy now had a daughter who was written about in newspapers and magazines. Roy had made himself quite unpopular by hounding everyone he knew and some he did not, and pressing articles about his daughter under their noses. Visitors to the flat were dragged out to the kitchen to pay homage to the refrigerator door, a latter day shrine, where all the latest photos and newspaper articles about Lili were taped up.

On this day however, Lili as a topic of conversation was in competition with the swimming baths which were to be pulled down in one month's time to make way for a leisure centre with a gymnasium, squash courts, saunas, restaurants and three swimming pools. The prospect of losing their livelihood frightened Roy and Shirley. The fear was causing confusion and preventing them from taking steps to find alternative work.

The atmosphere among the staff was funereal. When Henry and Lili went downstairs they discovered that Lili's arrival created a welcome diversion. Bill and Mrs Wright, who between them had clocked up almost eighty years service at the baths, were conferring over a mop and bucket when they set eyes on the visiting star.

"It's the end of an institution. Seventy-nine years of swimming," Bill told her. "My dad used to bring me here when I was a nipper."

"I suppose," said Lili, "they won't use mops and buckets at the leisure centre. They will have moved beyond it."

119

"Right," said Henry, who by now had found his wheelchair. "It will be done by solar suction."

"I went to see your play," said Bill. He never understood anything Henry said.

"So did I," said Mrs Wright. "I said to my old man, if that's what you've got to do to get on, well you've got to do it. It's a tough business, I told him, you can't criticize her, that girl's been starving."

"She don't look too good now," said Bill.

"No, it's not your fault is it darlin'?" said Mrs Wright. "I mean you've got to earn a living. I mean," she stared into the murky depths of her bucket. "If they'd have me up there instead of doing this, I'd whip my clothes off in a minute."

"Do us a favour," said Bill casting his eye disappointedly up and down Mrs Wright's amorphous torso. "Me and Betty came to see the play about five weeks ago. We didn't come round afterwards because Betty thought you might be embarrassed. You know after dancing like that in the all together. Betty said she wouldn't want to see anyone afterwards if she'd done something like that. Betty's very sensitive. I told her you're too sensitive for your own good. So we went round Leicester Square. Bloody hell! The prices they charge! And then we saw this bloke standing in a little blank space in the road. They'd towed his motor away. Or maybe it had been pinched, he didn't know. I told him that's one of the dangers of going up west. You never know what they'll do to your motor. He'd been to see your play an' all. Me and Betty caught the tube to Balham and then we got a bus. You won't catch me takin' the van up there. Betty said what a palaver just to see a play."

"Anyway, getting back to the point," said Mrs Wright, "You've done your best. And I think your Mum and Dad are getting over it now." She produced a piece of paper for Lili to sign for her granddaughter.

"You don't have to do that if you don't want," said Bill, "Paul Newman doesn't. He says they always throw it away anyway."

"She's not Paul Newman," said Mrs Wright.

Lili signed her autograph and looked up to be confronted by

Mr Hollis, a history teacher who also gave lessons in remedial swimming. He inquired after the play and then offered a method of absolution.

"You should do something classical. It will help erase the image," he told her and then headed off to the small pool.

"When I used to come here I was an unknown failure," Lili said to Henry as they moved to a quiet corner, "now I'm a famous failure."

"Not that famous," said Henry.

Dartey acknowledged that he had stayed in London in the summer months of 1984 because of the girl. Now he found that he was held in London by Africa itself.

It annoyed him to find that by remaining in London he had become one of DAF's prize plums sent hither and yon to serve the cause of that organization.

After returning from a conference in Geneva he was sent to New York where he had several meetings with DAF USA. A frequent topic of conversation was Bert Hahn.

"Is he a total asshole?" was a recurrent question thrown at Dartey. He found himself getting quite defensive on Hahn's behalf, telling his American counterparts that all Hahn's faults were due to being British.

After attending a meeting at the new United Nations Office for Emergency Operations in Africa, Dartey flew back to London and was drawn into another whirlwind of meetings and speeches. He tried to feed the new hunger for information about the African famine, a hunger which had been sharpened by emotional appeals recorded by rock stars. It was a situation he had to take advantage of while he could because the interest and concern would begin to wane. They would soon release all the extra helpers they had taken on at the DAF office and things would be back to normal.

Dartey did not offer consolation when he talked about the famine. He told people that throughout the disaster the West had acted too late and when they had acted there had been little co-ordination of effort. The aid programme had gone badly and was still going badly, largely because at the eleventh hour people had thrown food at the situation and very little money. The money was needed to pay for the transportation. Now that the rains had come in some areas, it was desperately important to get hundreds of tons of food to remote areas before the railway lines were unusable. They had enough food to sink Africa but few ways of getting it to the starving.

At some of the relief camps there were more children playing and less of them carried away in shrouds, but in the hills and remote areas small children were completely unprotected and without food. The extent of the famine was unimaginable.

No food aid or medicine was reaching over half of the hungry people in Ethiopia because of the civil war. Many were dying on the long trek to relief camps in the Sudan. Dartey was one of many who accused the Ethiopian government of using the famine as a means of repression against the people. Through his efforts and slightly behind Hahn's back DAF was now secretly funding food aid to the rebel-held areas of Ethiopia.

The extent of the crisis depressed Bert Hahn. It did not bend to the principles he had used in dealing with all other crises in his career. He could not encompass it. He had walked through a small part of it with Dartey, smelled it and touched it, and it had become part of him. As a form of consolation for himself he kept an album of photographs on his desk. The album showed people he had personally rescued. Chief among them were Berhanu and Zabish, pictured after they had been taken from Tekl el Bab to Kassala. Berhanu was now employed in the DAF compound at Kassala and Zabish was attending school there. Berhanu wanted to get back to Tigre now that the first rains had come and Dartey and Hahn were supplying money out of their own pockets to get him there. The album of Hahn's "personal triumphs" was shown to every visitor who came to his office and created a comforting diversion. The people in the album, he said, were his "adopted children".

Dartey avoided making visits to DAF headquarters in London whenever possible but occasionally circumstances forced him to show his face. A week after the dance in Suffolk he was required to attend a meeting there. He was surprised to see Lili Smith's brother sitting behind a desk stuffing envelopes and chatting to the girls. The young man caught sight of Dartey and then lowered his head as though trying to avoid any conversation.

Dartey spent two hours there. Every time he came downstairs to the front office he would see the young man's head dip on to his chest and concentrate on the serious business of stuffing envelopes. It was indecipherable behaviour. The presence of her brother reminded him of the hard won indifference he felt towards Lili Smith and that this indifference had transferred itself to his attitude towards all women.

A few nights later Dartey found himself giving another speech at yet another function to raise money for DAF. This was a dinner at the Basil Street Hotel in Knightsbridge. He looked at the heavily laden plates of the diners and wondered why an orgy of excess was deemed the best way to raise money for the starving.

He did not understand why people had to be compensated for giving to charity. Pop stars made records, actors put on shows, chefs prepared eight course dinners, all to tempt donations out of people. And beyond that was the old nagging question of what exactly giving did to Africa. In the emergency he had temporarily blinded his eye to that.

At midnight he came out of the Basil Street Hotel and walked down Sloane Street. The air was cold and damp after an hour of steady rain. Cars splashed puddles on to Dartey's fast deteriorating evening dress which was suffering combat fatigue on behalf of famine relief. He felt hungry. All that paté, salmon, sides of beef and mounds of out of season strawberries and he'd had nothing besides a glass of wine and a cup of coffee. He could not eat and give speeches. For him they were two mutually exclusive activities: his stomach would not allow it. Now he was relaxed and on his way to an all night café for a bacon sandwich.

He was pausing to see if he had any cash in his pockets when he heard footsteps running behind him, splashing in the puddles. He heard the slight panting of a woman out of breath, a sad, sighing noise. He knew before he turned round that it was her. His hunger immediately left him and was replaced by a sick indigestive sensation.

123

"Mr Dartey!"

He turned to behold Lili Smith running towards him wearing a long trench coat and a scarf over her head. Twice she went up to her ankles in a puddle but seemed oblivious as she charged onwards. When she caught up with him she stood breathing heavily and displaying a faceful of heavy make-up which had smudged in the rain. Rain seemed to be a constant in their relationhip. It had rained on their last meeting before he left for Africa. Her face had been uncluttered then. He wondered if the make-up was the remnants of some theatrical work. He did not want to know. His instinct was to run. He could easily outrun her and head off down Sloane Street, but he found himself standing there as though waiting for an execution.

"Well here I am." She blushed a deep red and her mascara aided by drops of rain travelled in slow rivulets down her cheeks.

Dartey said nothing.

"I wanted to see you," she added.

Dartey stared at her and saw that her face grew even redder.

"How did you know I was here?" he asked.

"It was in the paper . . . Are you going anywhere special?"

"Yes."

"Oh." She rubbed the rain off her face. "Can I walk along with you then?"

"What for?"

She did not answer but simply frowned and looked at her feet.

Dartey frowned and looked at his feet. Then he looked up and down Sloane Street carefully. Then he looked at the girl who, in spite of all the moisture in the air, was swallowing repeatedly as though trying to encourage some saliva into a dry mouth. She looked up and watched him anxiously as a dog might watch a cook in the kitchen.

A late bus went by and they both turned their heads to watch it with an intense interest. They continued to follow its course until it disappeared round the corner and went towards Hyde Park.

"I was going to get something to eat," he said finally.

She smiled nervously and shrugged her shoulders.

"All right then," he said almost inaudibly.

He headed towards his car which was parked in Pont Street. She walked in silence beside him.

When they reached the car she waited expectantly, not sure if she was going to be allowed in. Dartey climbed in and she stood on the pavement bending slightly so that she could see him. He leaned over and pushed the passenger door open. She sighed a small sigh of relief and almost fell into the car. The seat was damp from rain that had come through a leak in the roof but she seemed determinedly unaware of it.

"You're such a bloody actress," he said.

She looked indignant but said nothing.

Dartey drove to a workman's café near the DAF office in Westbourne Grove and ate his bacon sandwich while Lili Smith looked on.

"Aren't you hungry?"

"No", she said.

She leaned her head against an advertisement for Pepsi Cola and seemed like a regular customer, comfortable with the cracked formica tables and watery tomato ketchup. Under the bright lights of the café she looked almost repellent with her smudged, over made up face and wet hair straggling on her forehead.

"You're still acting?"

"Yes."

"What in?"

"The same thing you saw."

"The same play!"

"Yes I know. I can't believe it either. We had a terrible audience tonight. They coughed. I always take a cough as a personal affront."

She watched him eat the last of his bacon sandwich. He was not enjoying it; it was an act of will to eat it.

"Long runs play tricks on the mind," she continued. "They cause aberrant behaviour. That's probably why I'm behaving like this."

"Like what?"

"Pursuing you."

"This is aberrant behaviour?"

"I think so."

"Perhaps you're in the wrong profession." He finished the sandwich and pushed the plate away.

"I've practically died for it."

"That's no indication of a right choice. Want some coffee?"

The girl nodded. Dartey went to the counter and bought two thick, cracked cups of coffee which swilled in the saucer as he brought them to the table. They drank the coffee in silence. It was a ritual to mark the end of this encounter. He would drive her home and then escape.

It was still raining when they went outside and the rain did a pretty good job of removing the last of the mascara from the girl's cheeks.

"I'll take you to your place," Dartey said.

"I want to go home with you," she said firmly.

"No."

"Please," she grabbed his arm and looked at him not imploringly; it was a deadly serious, authoritative look.

Dartey drove home. The person sitting next to him in the car was not the one who had occupied his mind so effectively for so many months last year. What was it he had felt for her? Love? Or an impersonal passion that he could have dropped on anyone who happened to be there at the right time?

"It hasn't changed," she said as she walked into his flat, "except the sofa's gone."

"Were you counting on it?"

"No." She was not reacting to gibes, she was marching to her own tune. There was nothing he could do about it. She took off her scarf like someone planning to settle down for a while. Her wet hair clung to her head like a mould which she did not bother to rearrange or make more attractive. Knowing that not much hospitality would be forthcoming, she set off on a tour of the flat.

Walking round the living room she said, "I remember this."

Then she encircled the kitchen and went on to the bedroom. "I never went in here. But I could see it from the kitchen. It was always a mess."

Dartey leaned against the door and watched her walk around

126

the room which was half lit by a street lamp outside the window revealing an unmade bed or rather mattress, and a variety of shirts and socks on the floor. There was no furniture apart from the mattress. He had set up a rail to hang his clothes on: it revealed for her inspection that he had very few clothes. She studied the rack like somebody in a department store selecting a purchase. Then she went over to Dartey and kissed him, running her tongue along his lips. She paused to study the effect.

Dartey had known she would try something like this but he had not known how he would react. His face tightened and he almost spat out the words "All right!"

The girl winced slightly and backed away but he caught her and removed her coat. Then quickly and efficiently, like a nurse getting someone ready for a bath, he undressed her. In her nakedness she appeared surprisingly selfconscious for one who displayed her body nightly to the public. With a mixture of embarrassment and determination she unbuttoned his shirt and ran her fingers across his chest. Then she rested her cheek against him; he could feel her eyelashes brushing his skin.

At this point Dartey lost some of his medical detachment and pushed her down on to the bed. Sudden anger made the removal of his shoes, socks, trousers and underwear a far lengthier task than was necessary. But when he was eventually free of all barriers he threw himself on top of her. His anger drained her energy and she became non-combative, almost an observer. The process of love making proved to be far from it and was dispatched with fairly quickly.

Moments later they lay staring at the ceiling, removed from one another by this act. The branches of a tree waved across a street lamp outside the window and temporarily shrouded the room in a funereal darkness. Then the light returned but brought no relief. The two lay there for some time listening to the mournful sound of the wind outside.

In the half light they were visible but unseeing. They were as the dead, lost and with no hope, but also without care. If he had turned towards her Dartey would have seen the soft line of her hip, the jut of her knee, the white toes with flashes of painted

127

nails alongside his large sunburned feet. But Dartey saw nothing. He felt nothing. He did not even feel the anger.

Finally the girl turned towards him and engaged his attention. She gave him a stiff smile.

"Well . . ." She spoke almost brightly. She got out of bed and began searching through piles of clothing on the carpet. Dartey knew that she had withdrawn inside herself, reverting back to the self-contained typist he remembered, a typist who was at this moment on her hands and knees searching for her underwear.

He needed to get out of the vacuity of that room. He wandered out to the bathroom and looked at himself in the mirror. A slightly manic look in the eye, he thought. Then he went into the kitchen. The fluorescent lighting there was harsh and clear and made the situation in the bedroom seem more unreal.

He walked around idly looking for some wine which he knew was not there. He used to have some whisky in a cabinet but the cleaning lady had stolen it. He found a half-filled bottle of tonic water and threw it away. There was no comfort to be had in the kitchen. He did not know what to do about Lili Smith now. Without the anger to sustain him he was bereft of an attitude. Her deviousness, which before seemed so threatening, now appeared to be self-destructive.

He went back to the bedroom and found her still hunting her underwear in a desultory almost paralysed way.

"No luck?" he inquired cordially as though talking to an old fisherman on a bridge.

"No." Her voice was muffled under her hair which covered her face. All he could see of her was the long curve of her back, which looked like sculpted, deathly white marble.

A small feeling of kindness, a need to comfort her was a new and faint emotion which crept into the vacuum around him. It was a seeping emotion and one that was dangerous for him. He had enough sense to detect it immediately and destroy it.

A cloud moved and revealed a moon which hovered like a ball of white phosphorus alongside the street lamp outside the window. With the additional light came the conviction that he was totally safe, or rather that he had the capacity within himself to be totally safe. He would not slip into the quicksands of Lili Smith ever again, thank God.

Henry was getting fed up with his wheelchair. For a start it offended his sense of aesthetics. It was drab, steely and totally without sex appeal. He had felt distinctly at a disadvantage sitting in that obnoxious contraption among all the pretty women at DAF headquarters. This would no longer be a problem because he had been fired by DAF. His help was not needed now that the African famine was out of the headlines and the flow of contributions had ebbed considerably.

He was left with the wheelchair problem. There was something surgical in its appearance. It was as appealing as a dentist's chair or lift hauling apparatus. It had the impersonality of a hospital bathroom or a half-empty bottle of vinegar.

He was led to construct small models of streamlined racing wheelchairs out of strips of metal and toy car wheels and with bright splashes of colour he drew pictures of something that looked like a winged chariot. It could be folded with just a flick of the wrist, yet was light enough to be lifted by a child and was of course very beautiful. It was the ideal wheelchair: he called it the "Superoller".

The man at the local bicycle shop who made racing bicycles looked at Henry's models and drawings and told him the whole idea was structurally impossible. Henry tried to persuade him that there was money in wheelchairs, that there were thousands of potential buyers waiting to be released from the confines of their drab old chairs and that if he would only build a wheelchair according to Henry's specifications then the sky would be the limit. They could corner the European market and the American. And what about the Japanese? But the man just shook his head and said, "You'd have more luck trying to walk than getting one of them things together."

Henry went back home and retired to his bedroom. He was avoiding Roy and Shirley during the latter days of the Berkeley Road Baths. Nearly everything they said began with, "This is the last time . . ." "This is the last time the laundry will deliver the towels." "This is the last time there'll be a polo game in the big pool." "This is the last time I'll buy digestive biscuits for Bill and Mrs Wright." Henry chose to remove himself from this morbidity as much as possible and consider the next chapter of the book.

He had reached a little impasse as Lili was strangely silent. He had heard nothing from her since her last morose visit home. He had written to her and phoned several times but she was never in. He had even phoned the theatre one evening just before the half but Lili had not yet arrived. This was strangely out of character: she was one of those conscientious actresses who arrived at least an hour before every performance.

Last year Lili had been incommunicado for several months because of a long period of unemployment and depression. But now she was employed and if not wildly happy about it she was not inconsolable. She was a little morose last time he saw her but surely she couldn't sink into a depression merely because Mr Dartey had been rude to her on the phone. Whatever it was, Lili wasn't writing the letters any more and Henry was mystified.

The day after the Berkeley Road Baths closed, the funereal atmosphere crescendoed to an unbearable level. Henry escaped and went up to London to track down Lili. He caught the 52 bus from Victoria Station to Notting Hill Gate and imagined the splendid exit he would have made from the bus if only he had his classic Superoller. He did not believe that it was structurally impossible. Perhaps he would have to make a simpler drawing to show the man in the bicycle shop. He had to do something with himself now that he had been thrown out of DAF and Lili wasn't writing the letters.

He had enjoyed his days of employment, his first job, even if it was only stuffing envelopes. It was for a good cause and he was secretly, and very quietly in love with one of the girls there, a jolly plump person called Bibi. She had taken quite an interest in Henry. He had responded cautiously as it was always difficult for him to know if women were genuinely interested or just being kind. Now that he did not see her every day he missed her.

He indulged himself in quiet fantasies in which he would

speed up to Bibi in his Superoller, skid to a halt and sweep her off her feet; but they were doomed to remain fantasies, at least until he could persuade the man in the bicycle shop to take him seriously. He was dependent on this man as he didn't know anyone else who constructed things with wheels on.

A cherry tree was in full blossom in Charlie's front garden. One of his cats was sitting in the branches staring at Sunday afternoon strollers and looking particularly fetching as though posing for a calendar cover. The cat jumped down and followed Henry up to the front door.

Lili was some time coming after Henry rang the bell. He knew that she was there. He heard her voice and then there was a long silence. Eventually she appeared wearing a new dress with large puffed sleeves: it was a startling pink, a colour she had never worn before. Her hair had reverted to the strawberry blonde shade she had as a child. She wore no shoes.

"Henry!"

"Just passing."

"This is incredible Henry!"

Lili was as capable as anyone else of being falsely effusive but never to Henry. Her enthusiasm came at him like a rebuke. Her face had a softened appearance like a piece of putty that had been gently pressed by the palm of a hand and her skin was flushed and pretty.

"This is such a coincidence," she said. "I haven't been here all week. How did you know I'd be here?"

"Because I didn't know you wouldn't be."

Henry manoeuvred himself through the front door and followed Lili down the hallway to the kitchen.

"I'm going to New York in July. It's official!" Lili stopped and did a little tap dance.

"Incredible. How long have you known?"

"Oh—er couple of weeks." She sounded guilty.

"Congratulations! That's fantastic!" Henry knew there was no law that said Lili had to tell him everything about herself as soon as it happened. He felt hurt but he wasn't about to show it.

A man was sitting in the kitchen. Henry was bending his head trying to get his wheelchair untangled from an umbrella

131

stand but from this angle he could see that the man's shirt was only half tucked into his trousers and that he was barefoot like Lili. He looked up and saw that it was Mr Dartey.

Mr Dartey gave him a half smile and a nod.

"Hello," said Henry as casually as he could manage. "I won't stay long."

"Don't be daft. You've come all this way," said Lili.

"They're all practically suicidal. I had to get away."

Dartey nodded as if he understood. Lili must have told him about the closing of the Berkeley Road Baths. They must have had a conversation. More than a conversation, much more. They were like two sticks of sealing wax pushed together over a candle. Even though they were not looking at each other and Lili was pottering about making coffee, Henry sensed a sort of fusion between them. This was above and beyond the sensual warmth that filled the air like a heavily sprayed deodorant rendering it somewhat claustrophobic. It was not entirely unpleasant but it was exclusive.

For the first time ever Henry experienced a sense of separateness from Lili. For him it was like a real coming-of-age, something he had supposedly celebrated over a year ago. He accepted it right there and then, not without some anguish, but with a clear recognition that to do otherwise would be a complete waste of time.

Should he say something like, "You worked things out then" or, "I'm glad to see you're madly devoted lovers now"? Or should he go on pretending that it was perfectly normal for Mr Dartey to be sitting barefoot in Lili's kitchen on a Sunday morning with his shirt half hanging out?

He did neither, he just asked, "Where's Charlie?"

"Cardiff. Playing Bottom," said Lili handing him a cup of cappuccino. She also gave one to Mr Dartey. Henry noted that, of course, she didn't have to ask him whether he liked cappuccino.

Mr Dartey may have had endless conversations with Lili but he seemed fairly wordless now; he was far more chatty when Henry had met him on the train.

Henry felt a certain obligation to keep the conversation going.

"I'm working on a design for a new sort of wheelchair," he told them, "now that I've been thrown out of the DAF office."

"Thrown out!" Lili looked shocked.

"I told you about it Lili. I wrote to you."

Lili had the good grace to look upset and hung her head.

"I wouldn't mind so much. I mean it wasn't exactly a career maker, but there's this girl there I like . . ."

Mr Dartey leaned forward and opened his mouth as though about to offer a solution. But he changed his mind and sat back.

"What about the archery?" asked Lili.

"What about it?" replied Henry.

"You used to go to tournaments. I remember you went to one last year."

"Yes . . ." His head sank into his chest. He was aware that they would like to solve his problem quickly and move on.

"Following archery tournaments hither and yon can be expensive. I've been concentrating on earning some money."

Henry did not stay long and he was soon back on the 52 bus. At least, he thought gratefully, they weren't all over each other in his presence. He hated it when loving couples kissed and rubbed each other under his nose.

He noticed that Lili called him Dartey, not Edmund, Eddie or Ted, certainly not Mr Dartey anymore, just Dartey.

He was not sure that his visit had served any particular purpose. They seemed to have some difficulty in focusing upon his presence. He had felt at times as though he had dissolved into mist before their eyes or become a wallpaper pattern to which they gave a certain visual attention but little else.

Back in the gloom of the Berkeley Road Baths Henry helped with the packing. In a week they would move to a flat in Brighton. Roy had some idea of starting a business but it was a vague idea and would necessitate some sitting and thinking.

Henry did not feel that his future lay in Brighton but he saw no way of escape from it. Right now his future did not seem to lie anywhere. He felt cut off. He seemed to be growing older and nothing was happening. Was this it? Was this all he could expect?

Perhaps when Lili got over the first throes of passion she would start writing the letters again. But perhaps she wouldn't.

Perhaps she had moved on. He wasn't going to beg her to write them, so he would just have to sit and wait.

Dear Henry,

You looked like a bewildered worm on Sunday. You sat there waiting for an explanation and none was forthcoming. Sorry.

There is really nothing to explain. It's obvious isn't it? Dartey and I were taking turns to humiliate each other. Now we've stopped and I'm in a state of cautious bliss.

It's hard for me to remember why Dartey and I had such difficulty in communicating. We seem almost convivial now. I suppose underlying it somewhere is the knowledge that either one of us could return to being quite cruel; it's a little time bomb ticking away.

Dartey's a violent man with a meek exterior. Yesterday he kicked a car driven by four thuggish looking men because the car came over the edge of the curb when it turned the corner and came near us. The car slowed down after receiving this kick but Dartey just stood there bristling with a much larger fury than was necessary for the occasion and the men, seeing this, drove off. I suppose they didn't want to get involved with a six feet three inch maniac.

His fury is bubbling away below the surface waiting to have some of its pressure relieved occasionally and bursts out at any small excuse. I am sometimes that small excuse but if he shouts I shout back and it ends quickly.

I am really excited about going to New York. New York, New York! I always knew I would go there one day. It's a dream, a fantasy! I wish I was going with another play but this will have to do. I will pour my soul into it. I'll set the town alight with my great vision.

I have no idea what the Americans will make of this play. Dartey says they will equate the gloom of the story and the constant motion with drama. He's been to see the play twice lately (isn't that devotion for you?) and he says that the play is entirely different from the one he saw in Clapham, that Ian has managed to obfuscate the lack of dramatic content and structure with an almost demonic skill.

Dartey still asks me why I do the acting. I find myself trying to explain and he just looks at me in amazement. He still doesn't understand why.

We spend a lot of time talking about that and Africa. He's really tormented about the troubles in Africa, in fact they almost entirely occupy his mind. I would say that the mental content of Dartey amounts to forebodings about Africa and the current passion for me. There's nothing else. He doesn't think about what to eat for breakfast, gossip, smart cars or the best wine. He knows nothing about wine. You could give him vinegar and he wouldn't know the difference.

His mind is incredibly simple and uncluttered. Until he met me he thought solely about Africa. Now he's fitted me in there somewhere. He has to be reminded to eat. He's not so much a dreamer as a concentrater. He just concentrates and some of the time he concentrates on me.

My mind leaps about a great deal and Dartey's mind bores deep wells. We seem to communicate quite well in spite of this structural difficulty. The necessity to act, to flaunt oneself in public, is now getting the full force of Dartey's attention. He has a mind which likes solutions. No wonder Africa is driving him crazy and now this will too.

We have even discussed marriage. I am of the "it's just a piece of paper" school of thought but Dartey says living together is childish and uncommitted. You either do or you don't as far as he's concerned. Nevertheless I am currently spending most of my time at his flat.

You have been rather uncommunicative lately, Henry. When are you going to write to me again?

Love,
Lili

Dear Lili,

I have written to you several times. You just haven't noticed. Here's hoping you actually remember this one.

The move to Brighton was not too traumatic, though Mrs Wright and Bill got teary-eyed and a lot of the old regulars came to wave us off. The elderly bleached blonde who wears the nose and ear plugs gave the parents a china figurine which I will have to destroy. Somebody from the council gave our father some sort of certificate and several of the shops in the High Street sent something over. So we set off absolutely loaded with gifts.

Now we're here and the flat's all right but it lacks excitement. Do you think you could manage a quick trip to Brighton before you leave for New York? The parents are feeling a little alienated among the amusement arcades and fish and chips and you are a constant topic of conversation.

They are supposedly taking a month's holiday to allow the wounds to heal but how they plan to recover is beyond me. They are totally without resources for recreation. They're so wired up for working that they don't know how to do nothing. Living with them is like being locked in a room with two disturbed wasps.

Your going to New York is something they cling to, an achievement.

And of course it'll be really useful for the book. All the best theatrical biographies have a New York sequence.

As for the Dartey situation. Well . . . phew, what can I say? Sitting there in the kitchen he looked like a rogue elephant who'd made up his mind to really enjoy the captive life. I stand in awe of the whole thing.

Love,
Henry

Dear Lili,

Don't tell Henry I've written but could you come down and
see him before you go to New York?

He's having a bit of a hard time now that he's been thrown
out of that job in London. He hides in his room a lot and he
seems depressed. I really don't know why someone won't give
him a job.

You mean so much to him Lili. He just lives for your letters.
How about coming down next Sunday?

Love from your dear old mother,

Shirley

In order to develop a third world society a developer has to
exploit two elemental emotions—greed and shame. In order to
relate to a female a man has to succumb to a good degree of
carnality. Dartey was unconvinced that the means justified the
ends in the former but was now completely turned around in
his opinions about the latter.

Lili and he had become friends. He was beginning to
discover that what he had most distrusted in her was his own
overwhelming feeling. And now that he was beginning to know
Lili he found that her intensity and self involvement, two
qualities which might have repelled most men, were qualities
which completely matched his own. They were qualities that
made her self sufficient and completely unaware of what most
women expected of men. She did not lean on him, she did not
ask for advice, she did not seem to need him in the way that
females had in the past. He had spent his life running away
from needy women.

He realized that she had trapped him. That miserable fiasco
in his bedroom was not what it appeared to be on the surface. It
seemed to him at the time that she looked pathetic crawling
around naked looking for her underwear. But it was probably a
performance. She had probably planned for him to be angry
and for her to look pathetic. The smitten Dartey had suddenly

realised that if it was a performance, he appreciated the effort.

He had grabbed hold of her wrist and said, "Don't go." Of course the skin around her wrist reddened immediately.

"It's almost two o'clock," she said.

"We've got to talk."

"What about?"

"Anything."

"I didn't think you liked talking."

"I'll make a special dispensation for you."

Ignoring that, she had started to get dressed.

"I want you to stay the night," he said.

"Is that an order?"

"Yes if you like."

She went on dressing and seemed not to be considering the idea. She dressed in a shy manner, almost like somebody on a public beach. Then when she had her coat on, buttoned up, she sat down on the bed and said, "I didn't bring a toothbrush."

"You can borrow mine."

"That's not very hygienic."

"After what we've been up to it will hardly matter."

The tears had gone. She was looking almost beautiful; she could go from ugly to beautiful very quickly. And she had that disdainful look in her eye that came when she knew she had the upper hand.

"I could," she said, "even fit in a little typing for you in the morning."

"Don't bother. You're the worst typist I've ever had."

Later on with a great surge of wit she had asked him if he had all his typists and he had said only if they couldn't type.

Lili was an odd, uncomfortable woman who could very likely make the average man really miserable, but she was perfect for him. Dartey was intrigued to discover that a fairly mindless passion had led him to such perfection. Had there been some unseen intelligence in this mindlessness which gave him an amazing insight into a woman's character? Or had he been a puppet of some higher plan? Or was it just the luck of the draw? He didn't know. It was a mystery to him.

Lili Smith had become overnight a friend, a flat mate, a sort of wife. He had never lived with a woman before. He had always felt uneasy when a woman was still there in the morning, looking either predatory or prospective.

Now he had accepted the whole package without a murmur. The sudden little compromises, the sharing of space, the subtle confinement. He wanted Lili forever and he would do whatever was required to keep her. They had discussed marriage. He had tried to express to Lili, so far with no particular success, that marriage was a daring leap, the ultimate commitment of self. Lili saw that as a romantic delusion. It was still in the discussion stage.

"An actress?" his mother asked.

"Yes."

"That girl who used to eat the doughnuts every morning?"

"Yes."

"I expect she's had quite a varied life."

"Yes."

"I suppose I'd better ask her to dinner."

"That's up to you."

"What does she eat besides doughnuts?"

The dinner with Catherine Dartey was conspicuous for two reasons. One, it was the first one she had given without the help of Gabrielle and two, out of some peculiar perversity Lili chose to wear the black dress she had worn almost every day during her short life as a typist.

Catherine, equally perverse or perhaps for old times' sake, said, "What a lovely dress."

And Lili smiled graciously. Lili and Catherine smiled at each other a great deal.

His mother, Dartey noted, completely ignored him at the dinner and addressed all her remarks to Lili. It was as if she were obsessed with Lili and was afraid to let her out of her sight. She told Lili intimate details of her life, particularly of her plan to have six children which was thwarted by two miscarriages after the birth of Edmund and the subsequent death of her husband. Lili listened attentively and said very little about herself. Catherine, though, gave her a pretty thorough interrogation over the cheese and celery. Dartey recalled that it had been Catherine who originally interviewed Lili about the typing job. Then the questions must have concerned words per minute, now they centred on background and the direction of her work in the theatre.

Dartey was left to converse with the only other guest, William Pope, an elderly horticulturist who had been a friend of his father. The man reminded him of his father and had some of the artlessness and the gentleness he associated with people who devoted their life to soil and plants. As though testing William's goodness Dartey found himself complaining to him about the wives of DAF workers in Africa.

"They go out to suffer for a good cause but they end up comparing notes about servants and swimming pools."

"No point in suffering if you don't have to."

Dartey would not let William off lightly. He told him that development was a gestalt, a mental phenomenon of the Western mind and therefore irrelevant in the African experience. Projects, he said, were created to give DAF workers jobs.

"But everybody benefits." William manoeuvred a morsel of Stilton on to a cracker. Even this was done in a kindly manner.

"No they don't. Most experts spend a couple of years researching a project and then they go home about a year later leaving everything up in the air. Then another expert goes out and starts the research from scratch . . . Africa's plagued by people doing research."

For a mere second Catherine stopped talking to Lili and glanced over at her son anxiously.

At the same time Lili shook back a gloriously abandoned mess of red-gold hair, and smiled at Dartey.

Dartey sat back in his chair transfixed by this waving sea of hair and let the subject go.

"She's going to New York," his mother said when she phoned him the next day. He noticed that Catherine would now only phone him in the evening when Lili was at the theatre.

"Yes she is."

"Are you going?"

"I don't know."

"You're going to turn into a stage door Johnny."

"I doubt it."

"You will if you go to New York."

Dartey did not answer.

"She's sarcastic," Catherine went on. "Haven't you noticed that?"

"No I haven't."

"No you wouldn't. You have your head in the clouds."

Dartey found it difficult to listen to his mother. He had never really listened to her. As a small boy he had taken on the responsibility, left him by a dead father, to keep his mother safe and well. Early on he had sensed that his mother and he had little in common and he kept a civil, dutiful relationship with her, without revealing anything of himself. It had left his mother with the impression that he was saintly and devoted with none of the imperfections of the rest of humanity.

Two nights after the dinner party Catherine slipped out and, in the interests of research, saw Lili's play.

She was on the phone to Dartey the next evening.

"Well, I've seen it."

"Seen what?"

"Her play."

"Oh yes."

"Do you want to know what I think?"

"Of course."

"She's not very stable."

"Who is?"

"Well if you're going to be involved with a woman, that's important."

"Uh huh."

"I don't think she's worth more than a little affair. That's all I'm saying. Don't get serious."

Dartey did not argue with his mother. He had never argued with her. He humoured her.

Dear Lili,

It was great to see you yesterday. The parents were bowled over when you walked in with Dartey and now our mother is completely smitten. She keeps on saying, "Did you see his eyes?" and "He looks like a Greek god." I've never seen her giggle and twitter as much as she did around Dartey. I was afraid she was going to start squeezing him like someone testing a loaf.

You didn't tell me he drove a battered Honda Civic. You've really been most unspecific about the car. It's the last thing I imagined he'd drive. Our father is a bit worried about it. He says it's a shame he can't afford something better. And he figures Dartey doesn't make much from the aid business or from books about crop yields. He wants to know how many copies he's sold.

I thought Dartey stood up to them pretty well. He was very quiet. I don't think he's so much shy as that he doesn't have the faintest idea what to say. But who would around the parents?

The next chapter of the book is entitled "The Ascending Star. Lili in New York." It's a bit crass but it grabs the attention.

Bon voyage and good luck. You're going to be great!

Love,
Henry

P.S. The parents are dead serious about their threat to come to the first night.

P.P.S. "You don't look like your old self Henry." You must have said that about ten times. I think I look fine so don't start fussing. I'm a bit lethargic but I'll soon get over that.

Dear Lili,

You told Henry about my last letter and he's made me promise not to write about him any more. So, really Lili, *don't* tell him about this one.

Your visit did him the world of good. I don't think he's severely ill or anything like that. There's nothing wrong with Henry that a bit of activity wouldn't put right. Roy says it's a combination of everything that's got him down—getting fired, missing all the activity at Berkeley Road, and you getting all wrapped up in your Dartey. (And I'm not blaming you for that, Lili. I might run off with him myself.)

All I'm saying is keep on writing to Henry when you're in New York even if he doesn't write back.

See you on your first night.

Love from
Shirley

Dear Mr Hahn,

You may have been informed recently that Edmund Dartey is planning to give up his work for DAF and start a career in the entertainment business as personal manager to the actress Lili Smith.

I would like to inform you that this is merely a rumour put out by Miss Smith based on wishful thinking and is not in fact a reality.

You may rest assured that Mr Dartey will continue his good work with your organization.

Sincerely,
Catherine Dartey

"Hello."

"Yes."

"I've just heard from Bert Hahn. Apparently you wrote him a strange letter."

"No I didn't."

"You wrote to him."

"Yes I wrote to him."

"Well Mother, what made you do that?"

"I just wrote to him."

"But why did you write those things Mother?"

"What things?"

"The things you wrote."

"I don't know what you're talking about."

"You wrote a very strange letter."

"No I didn't."

"You did."

"I didn't."

"Are you disturbed about anything?"

"No."

"Then why did you write a letter like that? I have to go and see Hahn and clear the whole thing up."

"There's nothing to clear up."

"Yes there is."

"No there isn't."

"Those things weren't true Mother."

"What things?"

"The things you wrote in the letter!"

"Don't shout."

"Well what do you expect?"

"I don't know why you're getting so upset."

"I'm getting upset because you wrote a letter to Bert Hahn making wild statements that were completely unfounded."

"No they weren't."

"Of course they were. What's wrong with you?"

"You said you were unhappy working for DAF."

"Unhappy? When have I told you I'm unhappy?"

"You told William Pope."

"What?"

"At dinner the other night."

"That was just an idle chat mother."

"You said people who did your sort of research were wasting their time. I think she's made you lose interest in your work."

"I have not lost interest in my work."

"You said you have."

"Well I haven't . . . Look I know you're disturbed. But if you're worried about anything just tell me. Don't go writing letters about it. O.K.?"

"You're upset. You never used to get upset."

"I'm not upset!"

"Then why are you shouting? It worries me. You weren't like this before she came along."

PAUSE.

"Edmund are you still there?"

"Yes."

"Can you come round on Tuesday morning? I have to go to the specialist. My back is hurting again."

PAUSE.

"Well?"

"I don't know. I'm really busy. I'll see."

Dear Henry,

Well here I am! I can't believe I'm actually here. I'm living in a fifth floor walk up on West 82nd Street that belongs to a friend of Charlie's ex-wife. The friend is in Los Angeles and I have the whole enormous place to myself. It's big and white and I can see the Hudson River if I lean out of the window.

The apartment is full of cockroaches and has a pervading pungent sour smell of a chemical spray fatal to all cockroaches except the ones born in New York. They walk over and around the cockroach traps on the floor. They pop out of drawers and wave their little antennae disapprovingly. They are here, I suppose, to get me in a militant mood and ready for the daily battles on the streets. They must be one of the reasons all New Yorkers are so angry.

There are tall palms in the kitchen and bedroom and ficus trees in the bathroom with long leafy branches that tickle my back when I have a bath. There is a sky-light with iron bars across it and the door has a bar propped against it and four locks. To get out is a complicated enough procedure let alone getting in. It's like living in a high security greenhouse.

The first day I arrived the lavatory stopped flushing so I rushed out to a corner supermarket and bought some kitty litter. But a nice Chinese lady on the second floor gave me an elementary plumbing lesson and explained that I could flush the lavatory by pouring a bucket of water down it. It wasn't quite the ultra-ultra innovative experience I hoped to have on my first day in New York, but it was educational.

I'm rehearsing every day in a theatre on Fourth Street in Greenwich Village and will be getting $750 a week (less during rehearsals). Ian seems to have arrived in his spiritual home and is in a state of subdued ecstasy. He loves American coffee, American doughnuts and American actors, though he is finding that the latter ask far too many questions and have an intensity about the work that is considered a little too sweaty by British actors.

I love New York but I really miss Dartey. He's coming to the first night but that's three weeks away, three weeks . . . I'd thought that it might be nice to be on my own again but it's not. I feel almost ill with the misery of not seeing him.

We talk on the phone every day. Our phone bill would keep a family of five. But talking to a disembodied voice seems to increase the distance and makes me feel more isolated than ever.

Sometimes I wonder if I'm losing interest in my career because of Dartey or whether the loss of interest in my career was like a predatory animal that pounced on Dartey. I'm not sure, the mind is a complex thing and anyway I haven't really lost any interest in my work, I'm just powerfully distracted. My work is me. If I lose that there's nothing left to me.

I'm enjoying the rehearsals because I've escaped from David McNair. *He didn't come to New York.* Right up to the last minute he was coming but then something mysterious happened. Was it the money or the billing? Who knows? Ian is the only one who does know and he never tells me anything if he thinks I really want to know. All I know is that David McNair is no longer here casting a cloud of confusion over everything. He is the worst, most nonsensical actor I have ever worked with. The pain of working with him was increased by the fact that he had a large following and was approved of by most of the critics. But he's not here and I am. And I'll stay here as long as I don't faint away, pining after Dartey. Perhaps I'll dissolve into the sidewalks and they'll build a monument to me outside a doughnut shop in Greenwich Village.

The rest of the cast here are Americans struggling with British accents or they are British with green cards. The American actors are treating Ian with great respect probably because they don't understand what he is saying. After all, they've only had one week of rehearsal. Give them a few more days and they'll soon realize that nobody understands what Ian is saying.

On the first day he spent three hours lecturing us on the play as an assault, something that challenges the senses. He said that the New York production would lean more towards using the non-linear narrative rather than the traditional plot but would not incorporate those elements of the avant-garde which were merely right wing fads. Any complacency that had crept into the production would be eliminated. He finished off with an hour on the historic background of the play and its relevance to the Vietnam War.

Eleanor, our playwright who came over on People's Express, was convinced that he was talking about another play.

In actual material fact, what Ian has done with the New York production is to eliminate a lot more of the dialogue. Eleanor complains that it is "all just grunts and groans and songs now". Ian's attitude is "What are you complaining about love? I got your play to New York, didn't I?"

I have become Eleanor's confidante. This morning she said, "Ian says Americans aren't into words but everyone in New York talks all the time. They *love* words."

I said, "Perhaps Ian meant that although Americans talk a lot they don't listen, at least the ones who buy tickets to plays in New York."

There are, in fact, still quite a few words left, but Eleanor feels that if she weren't such a novice she would have had more control over Ian. "It's my experience," she keeps on telling me, "It happened to my family. I saw it as a play. I wrote it down. It was given to me. I heard it all. And I didn't hear any songs and dances."

I think Eleanor is working herself up for a rather late standoff with Ian, a sort of High Noon confrontation, when she will stride up on to the stage during rehearsals and shout, "No, you great big twit! You're not going to do that to my play."

147

An actor called Jason Parrish is playing Arthur Bailey. He is from Kansas City but has lived in New York for almost six years. You would love to watch him work, Henry, because he's a really interesting case. He's incredibly intense and asks questions that are unanswerable to anyone except Ian, who refuses to be fazed by anything. This morning he asked, "What are the Freudian implications of hanging?" He needed to know this for the scene where he goes into a café after he gets out of prison.

Ian said immediately, "The Freudian implications of hanging are many and varied and depend really upon the crimes attached to the hanging. And in your particular case, having been released from the death sentence, and having your first moments of freedom the effects would be fairly diffuse in your immediate experience." This seemed to satisfy Jason and he was able to go ahead with buying a cup of tea in the café.

Jason has read all sorts of books on British legal history and about Birmingham and has even looked into Eleanor's family tree. All this knowledge is hidden behind an extremely physical, almost sexual performance. He uses his body to express the meaning of the play and he's really trying to score in the part because it's his first job in six months. He's absolutely riveting as he never stops moving especially when I'm talking.

Jack Harter who's playing the MP is originally from Bradford. He doesn't scratch or pick his nose when I speak so I do the same for him. The language of the play comes easily to him and he concentrates on the meaning of the words themselves. He's done no research and he uses the rehearsal period to tell jokes and discuss good places for lunch. Is this what's thought of as a typical British actor?

After the first week of rehearsal Ian decided that as the second act of the play takes place during the war he would have two American servicemen in it. He had a quick discussion with the producer and then in the afternoon two delighted actors turned up. They are improvising their dialogue. Eleanor was not present at the rehearsal when these innovations were made: it was just her luck that she had arranged to go on a bus tour of the Bronx. By the time she got back the new members of the

148

cast had rehearsed their scenes twice and were cemented into the production. There was nothing she could do except mumble obscenities in my ear for a couple of hours.

One of the new actors is Frank Puritsky. He has an autocratic, stylish manner which must come from working as a waiter at a ritzy restaurant on the east side for the last decade. All his fellow waiters are in a state of shock because he has acquired an acting job. It's his first real job in three and a half years and he sees it as a complete miracle. It seems an incredible act of faith to hold on to the idea of being an actor when there is no outward proof of it for so long. Frank, like most actors, has that blind almost religious fervour which pulls him through the long dry periods. He has been rewarded with a few lines in Eleanor's bastardized creation, Ian's nudie-musical.

I have become something of a small star here, a minor twinkle. I have been interviewed several times and even went on a local television talk show. The interest is cautious. I will remain a minor twinkle and then, according to the direction of the reviews, whether favourable or guillotine, I will be hurled into darkest extinction or become a great light (or rather an off-Broadway light which is less luminous than a Broadway light but nevertheless quite incandescent).

Everyone here has horror stories of instant abandonment after getting bad press. Our producer said that within minutes of unfavourable reviews coming out for one of his plays he was left alone on a street corner by an entourage who had been around him for weeks, and he never saw any of them again.

New York is hot and sticky. The only air conditioner in the apartment is in the bedroom. I spend most of my time after work sitting on the bedroom floor with my chin on the window-sill hugging the air conditioner and thinking about Dartey. If you think this is a little dull, you could invent something more exciting for the book. Readers might have high expectations for the New York sequence.

Love,
Lili

P.S. Keep the faith Henry. Something good will happen. I

149

know it will. Once you get over the lethargy the whole world will explode.

"Hello."
    "Did I wake you up?"
    "No."
    "It's two in the morning."
    "You should be asleep."
    "Oh I'm sorry Dartey. I did wake you up, didn't I?"
    "No, no."
    "Well I won't keep you. I just wanted to say that your mother has phoned Ian a couple of times."
    "Oh God no."
    "Yes."
    "What did she say?"
    "Well Ian, you know him, if it doesn't directly concern him or the play he can't remember it. But it was some odd stuff about you coming to New York to manage my career."
    "Oh God."
    "How did she get his phone number?"
    "Oh she can do anything once she puts her mind to it."
    "Has she gone potty?"
    "Sort of. Well at least as far as this is concerned."
    "She told Ian that I was trying to destroy your career."
    "Oh God."
    PAUSE.
    "I don't really know how to deal with her. I can't stop her sweet ration or anything like that."
    "She doesn't like me does she?" (Small laugh.)
    "It's nothing to do with you Lili. It's all to do with me. Don't take it personally. I like you."
    "I think she has visions of you standing in my dressing room handing me my lipstick."
    "Oh who knows what goes on in her head . . . That's my alarm. I'm supposed to be in Oxford in an hour."
    "I'll phone you tonight."
    "I won't be back till late."

"Phone me when you get in then."
"It'll be about four in the morning your time."
"That's O.K."

The summer rains had followed on from the short spring rains in Wollo Province in Northern Ethiopia. They did not simply moisten the earth and refresh it with a gentle dew. Having been held back for so long in unseen regions the clouds now unleashed themselves with unrestrained force and bombarded the earth. The rain pushed the soil in heavy muddy sweeps into the Blue Nile where it travelled swiftly northwards, turning the water bright orange, and ended up as silt in Lake Nasser in Egypt.

In Philadelphia's John F. Kennedy Stadium thousands of parched overheated bodies were hosed down by firemen as they swayed in unison to the music at the Live Aid concert. But at Wembley Stadium in London the large majority of the hot sweaty crowd of seventy-two thousand received not the merest trickle of water, for security guards could only extend their hoses to a few lucky members of the audience near the stage.

In Sudan the deluge that had fallen from the skies had destroyed a bridge and the one rail link from Port Sudan to the famine areas further west. Thousands were left without hope.

Hath the rain a father? Or who hath begotten the drops of dew?

Out of whose womb came the ice? And the hoary frost of heaven, who hath gendered it?

The waters are hid as with a stone, and the face of the deep is frozen.

Canst thou bind the sweet influence of Pleiades, or loose the bands of Orion?

Canst thou bring forth Mazzaroth in his season? Or canst thou guide Arcturus with his sons?

Dartey stared at these verses which lay among the papers on his desk while a small television set in the corner provided noisy background music from the Live Aid concert at Wembley. The verses had been sent to DAF headquarters from a lady on the Isle of Man and forwarded to Dartey by a secretary who seemed to think that Bible verses were his particular province. "Difficult" letters were often dumped on him. Bert Hahn had once told him that he gave the appearance of being able to deal with anything. It was only an appearance. He had no idea what to say to the lady on the Isle of Man.

His attention drifted to the television. He marvelled at the awesome power of rock music that could turn thousands of individuals into one mindless mass and at the same time alert the whole world to a problem that had gone off the front pages.

He longed to be swept up in the general feeling of power and exultation and become convinced, as all those rock musicians and their happy audience seemed to be, that this day would wipe famine off the face of the earth. He longed to be crushed in that mass of seething bodies and blind himself to the dull realities which were spelled out in pedestrian language on papers all over his desk.

And then there were his Bible verses. "Canst thou bind the sweet influences of Pleiades?" It was a question that should have been sent to someone who had demonstrated a little more control in his life. He would send it back to DAF headquarters.

Intractable situations were closing in on Dartey. Lili was three thousand miles away, his mother was going a bit mad, and he had no idea what to do about that or anything else for that matter.

He could not discipline his mother. He had long ago passed that subtle turning point where the child became the parent, but Catherine had not passed this point with him: she lived in the past, she held on to the myth of her maternal authority as though Dartey were still a small boy. She was a queen who insisted on respect.

He had gone along with all that because it was a habit of years standing, because it would have required a strong emotional commitment to change and because to do otherwise would make Catherine unhappy.

But now things were different. On the surface it seemed to be a problem connected with Lili but obviously it was something beyond that. He had first noticed a change in his mother at the time of his last trip to Africa. She started to talk about death, his death, her death, how she could not cope if he died first. She was frightened that he would die in Africa. She had exhausted him with her fears of death.

She had been, as far as he could see, an exemplary mother up to that point. He really had nothing to compare her with but it seemed that she had been devoted and motherly in the right way, if there was a right way.

Two months after he returned from Africa, Gabrielle retired to go and live with her sister in Baden Baden. He was aware of the fact that Gabrielle's departure had been difficult for Catherine. It was possible that the loss of Gabrielle had triggered some sort of paranoia.

After Gabrielle his mother had employed a series of daily helps who did some cleaning and cooking. They were no substitute for Gabrielle. When they were in the house she sat in her bedroom until they had gone. She did not argue with them, she simply avoided them.

In the thirty years that she and Gabrielle had been together there had been daily battles, charges and counter charges; they were always on one side or another of an entanglement. Their raised voices were a constant household sound as accepted as the purr of a refrigerator or the ticking of a grandfather clock.

And now Gabrielle was gone and Catherine was in some sort of mourning. But why? How could the departure of an elderly cook affect his mother? She was only a cook after all, not a spouse.

He could not remember if his mother mourned unduly after his father's death. He could not remember how Catherine related to his father: he died before Dartey was old enough to really consider how people behaved towards each other. He remembered a quietness when his father was alive. His father never shouted so presumably there was little reason for his mother to shout. For it seemed to him that Catherine was not a dominating personality who set the tone of a relationship. She responded. She had responded to Gabrielle's pugnacious personality, and now obviously she was reacting to her loss.

And now he came to think of it, Catherine had never had any friends. She gave elaborate dinners to people on a list and was occasionally invited back but she had no friends. She used to stay home all day and argue with her cook.

Perhaps she had been completely fulfilled recoiling from Gabrielle's insults and thinking up retaliations. Was it a great passion of thirty years' standing? And if it was, who or what could fill the great void left by Gabrielle's departure? The wearying truth was that he was the prime and only candidate.

Dartey stood up from his desk and circled his head in a fruitless endeavor to remove the tension from his neck and shoulders. He missed Lili. Catherine's hostility to her was disturbing. Did she have the right to be hostile? What were the rights of motherhood? Was it an exalted position that gave a person a sort of diplomatic immunity to censure?

He had no idea. He went back to his reports on Northern Ethiopia. A success of sorts. The death rate there had been cut considerably. It was a comfort to know that DAF's work there had been effective. It gave him some strength to deal with the complete failure of DAF's efforts in Western Sudan where half a million people were expected to die.

Earlier in the year the relief organizations had divided up Sudan, a country the size of Western Europe, into manageable sections. DAF was having no more luck with its section than any other agency. Getting sacks of grain from Port Sudan to the western areas was a task that had already broken two DAF workers. One had gone slightly insane like his mother and the other had just disappeared. The trouble was the railway. A lot of people had chosen against their better judgment to assume that it would not break down and now that it had there were no alternative arrangements.

DAF workers spent long hours haggling with camel drivers who said they feared attacks by bands of the starving and demanded prohibitively high prices for their services. Haulage contractors suddenly doubled and trebled their charges. Trucks that actually did set out would be stuck for days in rain-soaked wadis. Frightening black storms would descend on any sort of transport and freeze it in its tracks. If a truck did get through to the outposts of the starving, local officials could choose to keep the grain in storage instead of distributing it. And then the final irony. By the time the rains were over and the piled up grain could reach the stricken areas it would swamp the local markets when the crops had just been harvested and damage a fragile economy.

On the television the bands played on as the night fell and the arc lights were switched on. Dartey found the last beer in the refrigerator and prepared himself for a long night at his desk. He was compiling notes for another book. It seemed that his anxiety about Africa increased when he was exiled from it. The book would be a long lament.

On Monday morning he took Catherine to the doctor. It was the third time he had taken her in a month. He felt that he had to do something for her as she did nothing but sit there all day waiting for him to visit. He felt a sense of dread as he went up the steps to her house, like a policeman going to tell a family about a traffic fatality. He would have to talk to her about her phone calls to New York.

Catherine was sweet and reposed, very much as she had always been when he was a child. She was exquisitely dressed in a cream silk suit and cream velour hat. It was almost as if he were a suitor.

"It's so good of you to come," she said in a little girl voice. "I know you're busy."

"How are you feeling?"

"In pain."

"Well let's go."

"Will you wait while I'm in there?"

"I'm not planning to abandon you."

"I thought I could take you out to lunch afterwards."

"No, sorry, I've got a lot of work to do."

"Oh . . . When are you going to New York?"

"Thursday." Dartey pretended not to see the hurt in her eyes.

"Is that her first night?"

"Yes it is."

"Well I'm sure you'll have a lovely time." Catherine managed a smile. It was a slightly cynical smile.

"Yes I expect I will."

Dartey took Catherine to see the specialist, waited and then brought her home. He did not confront her about the phone calls to New York. He had been disarmed by her child-like manner and thought it better not to attack her when she was in a generous mood. He felt relieved. He would handle it another day.

Beloved Parents,

I won't be able to meet you at the airport on Thursday as I'll be working all day. But just take a taxi to my apartment and ring the bell of 4D. The lady there will give you the keys to my apartment. There are five keys, you have to use three of them to unlock the door. It will take you about ten minutes to work it all out but be patient.

The tickets will be waiting for you at the box office. I'm sorry Henry's not coming. I hope it really is true that he's sticking around for a job possibility. But I have a feeling it's just pride and he won't come to New York until he can pay for himself.

I really hope that something good happens for Henry soon. I can't enjoy life when Henry's miserable. For some reason he's trying to keep up a front with me which he's never done before. You'll have to let me know how he's really getting on.

See you Thursday.

Love,
Lili

P.S. Dartey is coming to New York on Thursday too. Please try to remember that he's just an ordinary human being.

Dear Edmund,

It was nice of you to write but why ask me for help? I can't help you. But take my advice. Don't worry about your mother. You're just like your father and this is not good. She wore him out. When he died he was worn out and he was only a young man. Don't let her wear you out. I didn't put up with anything from her.

It is nice to be here. I make a jam sponge or biscuits every day for my sister's grandchildren and I sit on the lawn and look at the daisies. This is better than arguing about everything.

You were always a good boy so you have nothing to worry about.

Come to see me when you are in Baden Baden.

Gabrielle

THE NEW YORK TIMES

No one can accuse Eleanor Bright of leaning too heavily on the plot of *Help Me If You Can*. There's a certain valor in her determination to soldier on with complete disregard to the simplest rules of dramatic structure. Now on view at the Fourth Street Theater this production almost defies critical comment.

However taking a leaf out of Miss Bright's book I will wade on regardless. The story seems a familiar one; it could belong to one of those rugged films made in post-war Britain starring the young Richard Attenborough or Dirk Bogarde. It centers or rather meanders around Hilda Bailey (Lili Smith) whose husband has been unjustly accused of murder.

After an opening scene of pithy, working class dialogue, Miss Bright takes an acute right turn and drops into the household of a British Member of Parliament. One entire scene deals with a broken kitchen clock. The author has less assurance in portraying the upper classes and the characters here have a cardboard quality.

Those two threads are jerked together just before the end of the first act when Hilda Bailey goes to the M.P. and asks for help in proving her husband's innocence; he has been condemned to death and there is very little time to save him. Suddenly, we switch from kitchen clocks to an insidious seduction scene worthy of *Richard III*. Like poor Lady Anne, young Hilda is trapped by slimy and persuasive arguments. Jack Harter, freed from the constraints of the previous scene, gives a wonderfully reptilian performance as the M.P.

The act ends with an extraordinary dance by Miss Smith. Obviously burdened with the responsibility of expressing the quintessence of this somber play, Miss Smith removes her unattractive wartime garb and dances with a tragic fervor that is almost breathtaking.

The second act does not wind up the threads and we are left with many unanswered questions—not least the question why Hilda married her husband in the first place. As played by Jason Parrish he is a mean-spirited thug.

The lighting by Augustus Hill is spotty like the plot and the costumes designed by Jennifer Seal are unnecessarily unattractive and made one grateful to Miss Smith for removing them, though only marginally. Miss Smith is very thin. Ian Harding's direction is over compensatory and nervous but not without verve.

For all its faults, *Help Me If You Can* is not dull. It is bolstered by highly charged musical moments and provides if nothing else a distracting evening. Miss Bright's dialogue is unnervingly accurate when dealing with the working classes: listening to it is like being a fly on the wall in wartime England.

NEW YORK POST

There is something completely beguiling about Eleanor Bright's first play which opened last night at the Fourth Street Theater but it hints at much more.

What could be merely a simple drama about a wife struggling to save her husband from a death sentence becomes a complex metaphor for the fragility of life. The real action takes place in the subtext and is the nearest modern equivalent to a Chekhov play I've seen in a long time.

It is a play about standing alone against the forces of evil so it is aptly set in Britain at the beginning of the Second World War.

A young woman, Hilda Bailey, goes to a Member of Parliament to plead for his intervention in the unjust death sentence passed upon her husband. Lili Smith, an actress new to me, plays Hilda and introduces an odd angular charmer to the New York stage.

At the end of the first act we are presented with a seduction scene that is horrifying and disturbing. It has an almost satanic progression that is at times difficult to watch. And if that was not enough the scene is climaxed by one of the most dramatically intense dances I have ever seen on the stage. Hilda, as though pleading to the very forces of life, dances her heart out. There was not a breath in the theatre as Lili Smith danced. It was a profound and electrifying moment.

Jason Parrish as the doomed husband has the right balance of strength and insensitivity. Two G.I.'s, Frank Puritsky and Jeffrey Johnson, appear in the second act and add a welcome comic touch.

The lighting by Augustus Hill evokes the harsh no-nonsense world of wartime Britain and the costumes by Jennifer Seal are completely authentic.

The addition of music and songs has been used in exactly the right way, to express the feelings that could not come out in the spoken word. Ian Harding's direction follows the line of the piece and serves it in a complete and satisfying way. *Help Me If You Can* is a dramatic event.

Dear Henry,

Well there you go, two reviews for your perusal. People who attend first nights read reviews to find out what they saw (that's why critics explain the plot) and what they thought about it. Actors read reviews to find out what they did. Everybody else reads them to find out what to think in advance.

The *New York Times* critic's opinion is like the voice of God. What he doesn't like dies a miserable death. Why he has so much power is obviously some obscure but rigid collective decision by victims and perpetrator alike. We have no equivalent in London. It must have something to do with the difference between a parliamentary and a presidential form of government and their influence on theatrical meccas.

Everything that succeeds in New York commercial theatre must receive the seal of approval of the *Times* critic. As in all forms of dictatorship this is potentially extremely dangerous. The success or failure of the New York theatre hangs on the whims of one man and is subject to fluctuations of opinion caused by domestic problems, indigestion or whatever.

We are not sure if this voice of God pronounced final words of doom on our play. The few kind words at the end of his review have been carefully extracted and slapped up outside the theatre. They look perfectly respectable out of context. Large posters read: "Highly charged musical moments. A distracting evening. Unnervingly accurate. Jack Harter gives a wonderfully reptilian performance. Miss Smith dances with a tragic fervor that is almost breathtaking. *New York Times*."

Ian is convinced that the *Times* review had enough positive elements which, coupled with the rave from the *Post*, will get us through. On the strength of this conviction he has bought himself the most elaborate shiny black leather coat with buttons and zips all over made by a Japanese designer. He looks like an expensive handbag.

Dartey didn't come to the first night. His mother was taken ill and he had to drive her to hospital. Apparently she is all right now and he plans to come as soon as possible.

I felt terribly rejected when he didn't come, very hurt and miserable. I had a sneaking feeling that his mother was just

160

manipulating Dartey. He said that she was convulsed in agony with stomach pains and he couldn't possibly leave her: he thought it might be an ulcer or colitis and maybe he was right. Who am I to say?

Whatever it was, Dartey wasn't there on the first night and there's no law that says he should have been there; but I gave one of those performances that should be filmed and shown to student actors as a fine example of what not to do. Jason Parrish told me that at one point I actually did chew the scenery: I was standing by the upstage centre door crying and nibbling on the edge of the door. There are little teeth marks there to prove it.

The bad acting was like a disease lurking, waiting to be triggered off; all it needed was the electric atmosphere of a first night and the bad news from Dartey and out it all spewed. I was feeling sorry for myself, stepped out on to the stage, disengaged the mind and let the emotions take over. A lot of people who were either lying or didn't know any better congratulated me. But I swear to God I will never do that again. I couldn't live with myself.

My grim performance may have been responsible for the sombre note of the reviews; though not necessarily. Americans, I'm discovering, are serious, sentimental people and have a small gap in the place the rest of humanity store an ironic or satirical sense. That is except for Art Buchwald.

I dreamed last night that Dartey was sailing to a desert island with his mother. They were in a little pink boat that was letting in water, and they arrived on the shore just in time. As they climbed out of the boat it sank before their eyes. Dartey's mother was absolutely delighted and dragged him off along the beach to look for coconuts. I remember thinking that the expression on Dartey's face was hard to read and did not show his feelings about the sinking of the boat.

I really can't say that I know Dartey. He's still something of an enigma; and I certainly don't understand his mother. She's been behaving really strangely: she's phoned Ian several times and now he's beginning to look forward to her calls. They appeal to his twisted sense of humour. She tried to persuade him to replace me in the play because she thinks that it is my success that has trapped Dartey. It doesn't say much for her opinion of her son. According to Ian she said, "He wasn't interested in her when she was just a common little typist."

Ian can impersonate her voice now; he says he's going to get the wig and do it properly. After all those phone calls he sees the whole thing very clearly. He thinks that Dartey went to Africa to run away from his mother and that unless I'm prepared to go there too we haven't a hope in hell. But in fact the only safe route out for Dartey, in Ian's opinion, is to get involved in a nice homosexual relationship because then his mother won't get jealous.

I mentioned this to Dartey and he didn't seem very amused. He doesn't laugh about anything to do with his mother. He says he thinks her behaviour is connected with the retirement of Gabrielle, the cook. That may or may not be the case but whatever it is, he has no idea how to cope with it.

The whole thing really distresses him. He keeps on telling me that she hasn't always been like this and I suppose he's just waiting for her to get better. Meanwhile she's behaving atrociously. Some of her paranoia has flown across the Atlantic and I'm beginning to imagine that she and Dartey are conspiring together, that he agreed to stay in London to please her.

It was comforting to see the parents at the first night party beaming away and looking very English. I don't know quite what it is that makes the English look so very English; a slight pinkness of the skin perhaps, the gleeful politeness, and a sort of amazement that they actually got out of England. I never thought that I'd be so glad to see them. Feelings of abandonment made me rush across the room and fall on them; the surge of emotion lasted about ten minutes until our mother started tapping people on the shoulder and saying, "She's my daughter you know."

You were sadly missed Henry. I had been looking forward to seeing the frilly pink shirt and the natty black suit again. Come soon if you can. I can pay for the ticket. Please let me pay.

I'm settling down to the usual grind of eight performances a week. It's the same routine here as in London which has come as a little surprise. I somehow thought it would be touched with extra glamour in New York but there's very little difference. Admittedly the whole of Manhattan is out there, throbbing away all night long but to be honest I have no real desire to go out on the town every night—and if I did there's nobody in the company to go with.

Jason Parrish is on an exacting training schedule like an Olympic athlete. He has ballet classes at nine o'clock in the morning and then classes with Stella or Uta or Sandy, I'm not sure which. After that he has voice and sight singing classes. In between times he goes to Jack LaLanne's gym and rushes around on commercial auditions. So he has to go to bed early.

Jack Harter also goes to bed early because his wife has just had a baby and they've moved out to Queens. He says they're not getting any sleep as they're nervous parents. His wife was dreaming about a regular income and he was praying for a soap until this part came along. Now he's praying that the play will run forever.

I could possibly persuade Frank Puritsky to go out to dinner but all those years of working as a waiter have put him off eating in restaurants. And he's in litigation with his landlord at the moment which is draining a lot of spare energy. His landlord is trying to get rid of all the tenants and turn their building into a condominium. He cut off the heat in the winter and now refuses to carry out repairs. Frank has spent all his money on legal fees and is still nowhere near saving his apartment. If he loses his fixed rent he can't afford to live in New York.

One gets the impression that everything here is a battle and everyone is perpetually geared up for a fight. Frank says that when he used to leave the restaurant at 4 o'clock in the morning and go on the subway he dressed to look like a mugger. It's a good idea but not easy for everyone to achieve. I've tried it and always end up looking like someone wearing pyjamas underneath.

Life is really tough for an actor in New York. It's much too expensive and there are hardly any jobs. They are casting television stars instead of good actors in the theatre, film stars instead of television stars in television, and almost nobody gets a part in films nowadays except teenagers and machines.

I told my dresser about the book and she wants to be included in it. She's going to type up her bio for me to send to you. Her name is Debbie and she has blue and green hair and she's dying to be written about somewhere.

Debbie says that most actresses in New York get tired of working as cocktail waitresses and eventually marry well-to-do businessmen and move to Connecticut. I suppose Connecticut must be full of retired cocktail waitresses. Debbie says she will never move out there as she doesn't want to get bored and suburban.

I wonder if Dartey and I will ever get bored and suburban. I doubt it at this rate. We haven't seen each other for over a month. I'm still hugging the air conditioner in all my spare moments and right now I'm thinking about how easy it is to fake pains in the stomach. Do you remember I used to do it so that I wouldn't have to run through the showers at school? I didn't want to expose my naked body to the other girls. (Pause for a sigh of disbelief.)

The parents have gone home to Brighton fired up with new faith in mankind and trailing clouds of glory. So once again the acting has paid off in unexpected quarters.

Write soon Henry, I'm in desperate need of letters.

Love,
Lili

Part Four

LINWOOD COMPREHENSIVE SCHOOL

The Linwood Reporter
February 1986

Adrian Marshall

Last Friday Stacey Hennings, Jonathan Tree, Rebecca Binden and I went with Mr Buckley to interview Edmund Dartey for *The Linwood Reporter*. Two years ago Mr Dartey gave a series of Saturday talks at our school for the British African League. He knows a lot about the recent famine in Africa.

The thing I most liked about Mr Dartey was that he did not treat us like eleven-year-olds but talked to us as if we were grown-up reporters.

He said that he works for DAF which stands for development and food for the Third World, although sometimes he adds the T of Third World and calls it DAFT because a lot of the things DAF does are very daft indeed.

Aid organizations like DAF try to do good and help the Africans but for all sorts of reasons the work they do goes wrong quite often and causes harm. DAF works very hard to save lives in time of famine but some of the things it did in the past may have caused the famine. DAF workers try not to think about this because they enjoy working in Africa and don't want to go home.

167

DAF doesn't tell people about the things that go wrong because if they knew then they wouldn't give money to DAF.

Stacey Hennings

Mr Dartey is very tall with dark hair and lives near the canal in Little Venice in a flat with hardly any furniture in it. First of all he asked us what we knew about Africa and we told him not very much. Even though my ancestors must have come from Africa I don't know very much about their history because Africa's such a big place to learn about.

Mr Dartey said that if more people admitted that they didn't know enough about Africa then things might be better. People who go to help Africa are very well-intentioned but a lot of the things they do that seem to be good are really quite bad. For instance in the Sahel DAF engineers dig wells without consulting the local people. Sometimes aid agencies compete with each other to dig wells and do not get together to discuss it.

The people of the Sahel have a deep knowledge of how to use their land but outside interference has caused crowding of people into one place. If a well provides a lot of water hundreds of people will come and trample the ground instead of moving on from one place to the next as they have done for thousands of years. This causes what Mr Dartey called "desertification".

After our talk a lady brought us orange juice and biscuits. Mr Buckley told us she was an actress called Lili Smith who has been in a play in New York. She said that one day soon we could interview her for the Linwood Reporter too.

Jonathan Tree

I told Mr Dartey that I wanted to be a famine relief worker when I grow up. He said that relief workers are looked on as heroes so I would probably enjoy it and there would be plenty of work for me if things didn't change.

I asked how things could be changed and Mr Dartey said that aid work would have to be co-ordinated and a great deal of thought given to the reason for past failures. Because of its colonial past aid was originally given so that the donors could have political influence over African countries and aid was also given so that the Africans would not notice that they were being taken advantage of economically. Africa has sent away all the colonial masters but now they have more foreign experts in Africa than ever before and things are getting worse instead of better.

For aid to be of any use at all it must not be so secretive. People who give money must be told what is really going on and the people who are being helped must be asked what kind of help they would like. Aid workers mustn't think they know best.

Aid agencies are remarkably good at making their mistakes look all right to the general public and even to each other. This is because people who work for aid agencies think their work is very beneficial to mankind and therefore it doesn't matter if they tell lies. Mr Dartey says that it's more important to tell the truth because although people might not want to donate money when they hear the truth and some people might leave the agency, in the long run it would help the Third World more.

Rebecca Binden

It was really exciting going to interview Mr Dartey because we met the actress Lili Smith who I have seen on TV-am I told her I wanted to be an actress and she said I should think about it. She said most actors spend their lives being unemployed and trying to get a job and if I enjoyed the idea of that then it was definitely the life for me.

Mr Dartey told us a lot about the 1984 famine in Africa. I think we are so lucky we live in a country where there is enough to eat. I told Mr Dartey that we had been collecting money for Africa at school and he said it was good to collect money because Africa needed generosity. But, he said, we had been

169

misled by DAF and all the other aid organizations into thinking that enough money could help all the suffering people in Africa. This was a deception because the governments of Africa and the aid organizations know very well that this is impossible because of all the problems they have to deal with. Mr Dartey thought it would be helpful if DAF spent more time trying to explain these problems to everyone.

But DAF people are encouraged to write reports that make everybody feel happy and satisfied with DAF so it is hard to get at the truth.

Mr Dartey said that if we write down everything he told us then a lot of children would learn about aid to Africa. When we all grow up perhaps we will stop people taking advantage of Africa and let the African people work things out their own way.

I really liked going to see Mr Dartey because he was so interesting, but most of all I liked seeing Lili Smith because she has been on T.V. Next week she is going to America to make a film called *Help Me If You Can*. She has been in the play for a year in London and New York. She said that actors who play a part on the stage don't usually play the part in the film but she is going to do it. She doesn't know why but she is pleased about it anyway.

Dear Lili,

We can't believe it but Henry's finally agreed to get off his bottom and come out to see you. We're keeping our fingers crossed that a visit to Los Angeles might stir him up a bit. I know you're busy but try to keep an eye on him.

Roy says depressions can be something chemical and pills might help. But it's impossible to get Henry to see a doctor. Maybe you can talk him into seeing one of those fancy Californian doctors. You can get him to do anything.

Good luck with the film and save all your magazine and newspaper interviews for Roy. He's bought a gargantuan new album.

Don't forget there are such things as telephones.

Love,
Shirley

Dear Dartey,

Your interview with the children from Linwood Comprehensive School has been forwarded to me by the school's board
of governors. It read like a long suicide note. Why you should
find it necessary to unload your disagreements with DAF on to
a bunch of eleven-year-olds is beyond me.

You are obviously unhappy with DAF and I feel it only right
to put you out of your misery and let you go. I'm giving you
one month's notice. I think that will give you time to tie up all
the odds and ends.

Your seventeen years of service with DAF have been
remarkable. I'm only too aware that you are something of a
legend here which makes it doubly wretched for me to give you
this dismissal. But we can't accept disloyalty at DAF. You
must have been aware of the implications of the interview
beyond the school boundaries. I've already had an inquiry
from the London *Standard*.

I'm sorry it had to end like this.

Sincerely,
Bert Hahn

"So where are they filming today?" Henry asked.

"In a house in Reseda. It's a real dump. Supposed to be the
American equivalent of a council house in Birmingham. But it
looks like a real slum to me, like a knacker's yard. They have
junk all over the front lawn," said Eleanor Bright.

"Do they mind if you go to watch?"

"No. But I wouldn't bother if I were you. It's so boring. All you do is sit around all day and talk about your life while Lili walks up and down the path twenty times and then they break for lunch. It's not all it's cracked up to be."

Henry was sitting on a long white sofa in a chalet of the Bel Air Hotel in Los Angeles and noted with interest that there were matching white phones at either end of the sofa. There was also a phone next to the toilet roll in the bathroom and perhaps others strategically placed. He had only just arrived and had not investigated further than that yet.

Eleanor Bright was moving about the room in a small yellow and red bikini that showed far more of her stout body than was necessary for Henry's taste. The bikini looked like strips of ribbon tied round an inflatable mattress, a well-oiled, lobster-red mattress.

Through the window Henry could see the brightest of blue unblinking skies feathered with tropical vegetation below and a waiter wending his way up the path towards the chalet.

"Here he comes," announced Eleanor.

The waiter was wheeling a trolley laden with a cornucopia of exotic fruit and a variety of silver and crystal bowls that gave promise of a considerable banquet.

"My God Eleanor! All I wanted was a lemonade." Henry was still clutching the handle of his aeroplane carry-on luggage and was wearing the white trousers and bright Hawaiian shirt Shirley had bought especially for the trip. He had the dazed appearance of someone going up and down in a lift that wouldn't stop.

"This is the land of plenty, my son. Enjoy it." Eleanor walked to the door, her flabby bottom wobbling joyfully out of the small confines of the bikini.

The trolley was wheeled in and set alongside the dining room table. The waiter was transfixed by the sight of Henry, who threw aside the handle of his carry-on luggage, slid off the sofa and made his way briskly across the floor on his stomach. His goal was a can of Pepsi-Cola which he took from the lower shelf of the trolley and drank in one swig.

Henry plonked the can back on the trolley and wiped his mouth. "I was thirsty," he explained to the waiter who had forgotten to leave.

"He just got off the plane. It makes you thirsty," Eleanor explained further.

"Yes," said the waiter slowly. "Planes make you thirsty."

Eleanor sat down at the table and took a napkin. Henry's powerful, thick fingers locked on to the side of a straight backed chair and pulled his body into place on the chair. He sat like any slightly slumped individual with only the baggy almost empty trouser legs betraying anything less than normal.

The waiter gathered his wits about him, smiled awkwardly and left.

"I thought he'd never go," said Eleanor. "Now look, this is chicken salad with mayonnaise. They put mayonnaise on everything. But it's really good."

"What's that?"

"That's strawberry shortcake. They put cream on it because they couldn't put mayonnaise on it."

Henry turned to the mountain of grapes, melon, cherries, guava and papaya, heaved a deep sigh and took another Pepsi-Cola.

"I have closed my mind to the fourteen point four percent unemployment in Birmingham," said Eleanor popping a grape into her mouth.

"Isn't it more than that?"

"It's about fifty percent in my street. But I've closed my mind to it."

Eleanor had closed her mind to a great many things in order to enjoy her respite at the Bel Air Hotel. She had severe doubts about the humanity of the producers who had bought the rights to her play. She was going to get screen credit for the film along with two men who wore Nike Shoes and drove Mercedes sports cars; they had been hired to Americanize the piece but as far as Eleanor was concerned they had evaporated it. They made Ian Harding's attempt to metamorphose the play look amateur by comparison.

Eleanor had allowed herself one comment when she met Henry at the airport. "They've ruined it, love. I'll probably have a good cry when I see it on the screen. But other than that I want to forget about it."

She wanted to forget about it and it seemed as if she had. She

173

was being kept in grand style, ostensibly to work on last minute re-writes, but in actual practice she was never asked to make an appearance. While the other two writers chopped, fiddled with and largely replaced her words, she lay beside the swimming pool of the Bel Air Hotel and worked on counting her blessings.

"Fourteeen point four percent," Eleanor repeated, helping herself to a large dollop of strawberry shortcake. "I'm having this first. Treats first is my motto."

"Your new motto?" inquired Henry.

"Right. And I'm not going to diet until I get back to the fourteen point four percent."

Eleanor had turned into an instant Californian. She had met Henry at the airport wearing a tennis visor, red shorts and the bikini top. The worried flight officials who escorted Henry off the plane had expected to hand him over to a more responsibly dressed individual.

Throughout his journey Henry had spent a considerable amount of time trying to calm flight attendants and airport staff who were not accustomed to the sight of a wheelchair bound passenger travelling on his own. At Heathrow, when on two occasions it seemed as if he might be banned from the flight, he pointed to a man ahead of him and said "I'm with him". This was effective and he was able to board the plane. Once the plane had taken off there was nothing anyone could do to remove him.

When he crawled to the toilet he could not close the door while urinating. A passenger complained and a steward was summoned to hold a blanket across the doorway. Otherwise the flight went without incident until Eleanor arrived. "I think they wanted to see someone in a nurse's uniform," she said hitching up her bikini bra strap.

She dug a long silver spoon into the creamy mounds of strawberry shortcake while Henry sat and clutched his can of Pepsi-Cola. The effects of the long plane ride and a leap back eight hours in time made Henry's head feel as though it were floating through space. Occasionally Eleanor's voice became echo-like and distant and her large figure went in and out of focus.

He managed to remain alert while Eleanor, now dressed in a voluminous kaftan, took him on a tour of the hotel grounds. They paused on a small decorative bridge and watched swans floating serenely on the water beneath. It was an English country scene carved out of the dry Californian earth with its own special addition of gaudy desert plants and the ubiquitous palm tree.

They went to the car park and watched the valet parking. Casually dressed owners of Rolls Royce and Mercedes cars stepped out and gave their keys to young Mexicans who parked the cars in neat rows. Cars rolled in and rolled out. It was the best kind of theatre for Henry and Eleanor in their shared state of befuddlement—colourful, full of social contrast yet undemanding. It held their attention for some while.

As they watched a particularly spectacular brown and cream Rolls purr into place Eleanor broached the subject of Dartey. Was he coming to see Lili?

Henry had no idea.

"Always apart and every time they meet it's like a honeymoon." Eleanor thoroughly scrutinized a man in sunglasses and tennis shorts who stepped out of the Rolls. The man glanced up at the odd couple in the front row of the stalls. Henry and Eleanor stared back unabashed, completely entertained.

"Mind you," said Eleanor, "the danger is that you can get used to being on your own."

They left the parking lot and went to sit by the swimming pool where the long shadows of the late afternoon were stretching over the bright blue water and pool-side umbrellas. The sunbathers had left and it became a shady secret enclave for the two of them.

Eleanor sank back on to a soft lounge chair. "How's life Henry?"

It was a prohibitive question. Henry's mobile face tautened. He was suddenly a prisoner before the bench. "Fine," he said quickly, indicating that this was his final word on the issue. But Eleanor was not tuned in.

"Lili says your parents are going to open a tea shop."

"They keep on talking about it."

"And what are you going to do?"

"I have no idea." Henry turned his head away quickly and studied a poolside notice intently.

"And what made you come to L.A.? Lili said it's hard to get you to move."

"I came to do some research." Henry finished reading the notice and turned to face Eleanor. "I'm working on a biography of Lili." His lifeline, the book. When all else failed he always had the book. Its power to sustain him sometimes weakened but never completely died.

"You're a writer?"

"Of sorts. It's based on her letters but sometimes she forgets to write. The L.A. section was in danger of being a complete blank so I've come to do my own research." A slight bending of the truth. He had been coerced into coming to Los Angeles. Now he was here he might do some research.

"Research? What kind of research?"

"Oh I don't know really."

"Well what do you want? Local colour? Facts about the business? Gossip?"

"I think I'll just hang around. Could we go out to the set now?"

"No they'll be wrapping any minute. Lili might even be on her way now . . . Let's see, I could give you a few pointers. Do you want to know about agents?"

"Not really." Henry began to feel tired and faint.

"I have an agent called Bill Meyer who has an office on the fifteenth floor in Century City with about fifteen secretaries with long red nails, great big windows looking out over Beverly Hills, coffee machines all over the place. And expensive oriental paintings and rugs."

Eleanor's rubbery face melted and changed shape before Henry's jet-lagged eyes. For a mini-second he dropped into a deep sleep.

"He sends me out to pitch ideas."

"Who does?" Henry jiggled his chair backwards and forwards trying to shake some blood and oxygen towards his brain.

"Bill Meyer. You'd be good at pitching. You've got such

expressive eyes. You could hypnotize them. They'd love you."

"Have you had any luck?"

"No. Everyone tells me I'm an artist. That's like saying you've wet your pants, I mean, it's really unacceptable."

"Are you sure it's right for you to be here?"

Eleanor rearranged her kaftan. "My mother used to say, if you don't like it spit it out . . . I can't bring myself to spit it out."

It was almost midnight before Henry was driving towards Lili's home on Mulholland Drive. Lili sat beside him looking pale and thinner but she had not stopped grinning since she first caught sight of Henry lolling on Eleanor's white sofa.

"How's everything going?" she asked.

"Fine." Henry was too tired to be disturbed by the question.

"Have you had any more interviews?"

"God Lili you sound like our mother . . . Is Dartey coming?"

Lili stopped grinning. She sighed and looked out of the window at the late night traffic running along Sunset Boulevard. "I don't know. Dartey has some entanglements. I mean he isn't really unattached. I don't know if he ever will be."

She pressed her hands tightly over her eyes and then drew them down over her cheeks and chin as though trying to wipe off a coating of tiredness and misery.

"Oh God . . ."

Henry heard the words and he fought to make sense of them. He felt his sister's hand reach out to him in the darkness but when she turned towards him, Henry had fallen asleep.

Bert Hahn had accused Dartey of writing a suicide note. It had not felt that intentional but . . . perhaps it was.

Being thrown out of DAF was inevitable. Nobody was surprised, least of all Dartey, but it required a change of gear which was not as easy as he expected. The work for DAF had been a protection and now that it was beginning to wind down,

177

he was discovering what life was like without it. He was going to make one last trip to Africa under the auspices of DAF and then that was it. Without the immediate pressure of the usual busy work at DAF, the whole business with his mother and her neurosis became much more oppressive.

Catherine had continued to write those damn letters. She had fished around and acquired one or two useful addresses in Los Angeles. About a week after Lili had started work there those letters began dropping on her producer's desk, and in the offices of the *Hollywood Reporter* and the *Daily Variety*. They went in a large circle. Copies were sent to Lili and she sent them on to him. When he showed them to Catherine she always gave him that hurt long suffering look, that crucified look.

Dartey imagined that she must have spent hours researching what means were open to her, what channels she could take, what would be considered damaging to Lili. She was impressively resourceful. It was obviously fixed in her mind that if she could put a large dent in Lili's career then her relationship with her son would be safer. The idea was completely childish and illogical but it had given her a whole new career of her own. Her life used to be devoted to arguing with her cook, now it was spent on this diabolical research. It was therapeutic in that it kept her alert and busy. But could it be justified from the point of view of therapy?

Lili did not complain. He knew she wouldn't. There was no contract between them, but they had taken each other on for better or for worse. And the worse included obstreperous relatives. His mother's current behaviour was an impediment, a major obstacle really. They would share it together and live through it. His mother was sick and there was nothing he could do about it.

When Lili had come back from New York they had spent five weeks together. It had felt right. They should always be together. Now Lili had gone again but he had absolute faith that they could live through the prolonged absences and the assaults by his mother. It was an absolute, unshakeable faith.

Leaving DAF was a cleansing thing for him. He would tie all the loose ends up, he would go to Los Angeles and visit Lili and then . . . he would see.

In the meantime, what could he do about Catherine? He had a photocopy of one of her letters on his desk. It was typed. When had she learned to type? The letter had been sent to the producers of Lili's film suggesting that Lili had an alcohol and drugs problem. "Perhaps you should re-examine her medical insurance," said the letter.

He tried to remonstrate with his mother and explain that she was upsetting Lili. But he would always get that hurt look and more than hurt she would look confused as if she had no idea what he was talking about. It seemed as though he were attacking her. Sometimes she wept.

Once he swore at her and she packed her bags and went to Scotland for three days. It was another indication that she was treating their relationship as some sort of romantic affair. Lovers, not mothers, went off in a huff and sat in hotel rooms waiting to be coaxed back.

He did at one point persuade her to see a psychiatrist. After several visits the psychiatrist told Dartey that Catherine seemed to be a very charming woman who merely needed to get out of the house more often. He suggested charity work, getting involved in helping others. Catherine said she would not visit hospitals or prisons because they were so ugly and standing on a corner rattling a tin would make her back ache.

The indeterminate factor was Catherine's degree of responsibility. Did she know she was inflicting pain? Was it calculated? She seemed oblivious of her behaviour or its consequences, making it difficult to condemn her. Nevertheless she was committing a crime and getting away with it. Was this madness or was this the ultimate sanity?

Thank God Lili hadn't blown the whole thing out of proportion. She saw it as a childish misdemeanour, nothing to get upset about. Dartey felt tired; he had been thrown out of DAF after seventeen years. It was not unexpected but he needed to know that someone was on his side. Catherine was not. Thank God for Lili's good sense.

When he awoke on his first morning in Lili's hillside house

Henry found himself entirely alone. He wheeled his chair from room to room looking for some signs of life; he needed to apologise to Lili for falling asleep in the car. But she had gone to work and he would have to keep his apologies to himself.

He could see the glint of a swimming pool through a profusion of flowering vines that grew over the window. The flowers on the vine were a delicate shade of violet and threw tiny splashes of colour into the living room which was entirely white. White carpets, white lamps, white sofas and chairs, everything was softly and expensively white.

Henry found several bathrooms and a sauna. He crawled into the sauna to investigate and then could not get out as the door was heavy and the handle too high. Visions of being stuck in the sauna until Lili came home tormented him for several minutes. He could not remember why the door had been so easy to open when he crawled in. Finally he lassoed the door handle with his belt and pulled himself up to turn the knob.

When he came out of this tomb he discovered that there was somebody in the house.

A Mexican girl who could speak no English was making coffee in the kitchen. She smiled knowingly at Henry and pointed to a note on the counter. It read, "Eleanor will bring you to the set or take you to Disneyland if you'd prefer. Lili."

He went out on to the patio thinking that as soon as the Mexican girl had finished in the kitchen he would see if he could dig out some cornflakes. However, the girl brought coffee, fresh fruit and French toast and placed it on one of the patio tables.

"Mucho gracias," said Henry. The girl tittered.

Tall Italian cypresses waved in the distance and a white cat with bright blue eyes sat on a wall and studied Henry. He tried to remember what Lili had been saying when he fell asleep last night. She had such pain and fatigue in her voice. It was something about Dartey not being unattached. What did that mean? Was there an old girl friend in the background, a wife even?

The sky was just like the sky over the Bel Air Hotel: a bright unblinking blue without a single cloud. There were avocado and fig trees in the garden, and a small orchard of citrus trees, orange, lemon and grapefruit. The white cat jumped off the wall, gave Henry a suspicious glance, then went to drink some water out of the swimming pool.

The idea that the Dartey phase might be coming to an end was a blot on this paradise. He had devoted a good deal of the book to Dartey because he added texture to the story. He had felt that he would last and that by the time the book came out Dartey would still be around. If Dartey went it would mean changing the emphasis of the book.

He must have been wrong about Dartey. Perhaps Lili was going to live a solitary life, devoted entirely to her career. After all, that was what she had done so far. Lili had always said that she wasn't interested in being happy. He wondered if Dartey was.

What was his own idea of happiness? It was amazing that he could even ask himself that question. The last few months had been continual greyness, a sort of solitary confinement, and he hadn't asked himself any questions. He had refused to think. Why should he think when there wasn't any point to it? Now here he was sitting in paradise toying with his definition of happiness.

He had started to put his mind to Lili's biography again. For a while it had been hard to raise any enthusiasm for it, but now he had to justify his visit. The visit had arisen out of Roy and Shirley's fretfulness and his own increasing inertia. He had been booked on a flight and taken to the airport before he realized what was happening. The shock of finding himself at the airport had stirred him into action. He wanted to get past those doubtful officials simply because they were doubtful. After he had told the interesting lies about his companion nurse who had just gone through passport control and he had actually boarded the plane, he felt a wonderful sense of achievement.

Now it was clear that getting Lili's biography published would be as near happiness as he could imagine. And of course if he could find some way to manufacture his Superoller, well that would be the icing on the cake. The swimming pool water rippled and made him think of the Berkeley Road Baths and all those years when he used to astound everyone with his physical feats. They all said he would "go a long way".

The white cat seemed to sneer at him for having that thought. Then the cat's eyes suddenly opened wide as if something remarkable had happened. Well in a way something fairly noteworthy had happened. He had not been here twenty-four hours and already he had done a major piece of research.

By March 1986 donations to DAF had dropped considerably. Dartey's final task for DAF was to go on a ten day cost-cutting tour of all their nutrition-health centres in the Sahel. Dartey spent the ten days without a bath or shower, which was not an economy measure but merely unavoidable under the rather pressured circumstances.

He recalled that when he had visited their centre at Ajibar eighteen months before he had seen twenty-five corpses, mostly children, laid out in a tent, ready to be washed and wrapped in grain sacks. As a mother lay over her child screaming with grief, Hahn, he remembered, had wept. Twenty-five to fifty people were dying every night.

Now the children were mostly active and smiling. There had been only one reported death the night before. But the outlook was not all that rosy. In January the United Nations Office of Emergency Operations in Africa had projected that two years after the famine nineteen million would continue to get sick, starve and thirst. And it was a sad but inescapable fact that many children would die if the DAF trucks didn't roll up carrying high protein food mixtures. These children still had no other source of food.

Dartey went back to London without any suggestions for cutting costs except for his usual one, the one that was only too well known at DAF, that far more DAF personnel should be replaced by local people.

As his plane headed towards Heathrow Dartey could not shake off a sense of confusion. The chaos of Africa swirled around him like frothy white clouds. And there floating along with it like a small dark speck was his own personal chaos.

182

Only one thing was slowly becoming clear: he had been handling his mother with a misplaced sense of compassion. He began to see that she was behaving badly because he had done nothing to stop her. Then like a state of grace, complete clarity of mind descended upon him and he saw that if he did not prevent further attacks by his mother, he would lose Lili.

In his recent phone conversations with Lili she had sounded depressed and quiet. He had attributed this to tiredness and overworking; now he saw that he had not been reading the signs. He had been caught up in the drama of his sudden departure from DAF and had trusted to Lili's good sense and compassion as though it were a rock that they could all lean upon. But no one was that compassionate. The long absences had been difficult but not impossible. His mother had been impossible.

Up until now he had seen his mother's behaviour as an inescapable burden, something he had taken on by being her son. But he was beginning to see that an attack was an attack whatever the source and should be treated as such.

The phone was ringing as he walked in the door of his flat.

"Hello."

"Oh." A deep sigh of relief. "You're home."

"Yes, I just got in."

"Are you all right?"

"Yes I'm alive."

Catherine laughed. "Oh . . . I—er . . . well I got so worried. I can't see why you want to go on these trips!"

"It's my job. Or rather it was my job. Today's my last day with DAF." Dartey had avoided telling Catherine up until now. Even this avoidance he now saw as a sort of pandering to her fear.

"You're leaving DAF?"

"Yes I've been fired."

There was a pause, then Catherine said in a timid little voice, "Did she have anything to do with this?"

"No, Mother she didn't. You're the one who tries to get people fired."

There was a long pause. Dartey took the phone across the

room and began opening his mail. Finally Catherine spoke.

"I don't know what you mean."

"What the fuck do you think I mean?"

There was another long pause before she said, "It's just that I get so frightened."

"You're going to have to learn to keep your fear to yourself. And listen . . . Are you listening?"

"Don't shout."

"If you write one more of those letters, don't expect to see me again. Do you understand what I'm saying?"

Another interminable pause then, "Teddy, don't be so unkind."

She had not called him Teddy since he was a small boy. He had an immediate image of his mother, beautiful and immaculate, standing on the station at the end of the school term. And he, seven years old, overwhelmingly relieved to see her.

"I'm not being unkind." They could not stand on that station forever frozen in time.

"Well what are you going to do now? Have you got another job?"

"No."

"Oh dear."

"It's not your problem."

"How do you expect to make it not my problem?"

"Work on it."

Later in the day Dartey was struck with a few moments of remorse and felt that he should write a consoling letter to his troubled mother. But he realised it would be misinterpreted as approval and he dismissed the idea.

Notes for book by Henry Smith.

Film sets run according to a feudal system, the stars being chief among the feudal nobility and the camera crew, sparks, grips, hairdressers etc being happy serfs. When I first arrived on the set, being completely outside the system, I was largely ignored. As soon as it was discovered that I was Lili's brother and therefore of noble blood, I was given a baseball cap and a silky jacket with the film's name on it. My wheelchair became the centre of off-stage activity. I was in.

Everyone seems very happy with the feudal system, and although there is much complaint about pressure and lack of communication there is no revolutionary fervour.

When Lili appears there is a rustle of attention from every quarter. All the crew laugh loudly at her jokes and she watches them laughing. I think she tries to understand why they laugh so loudly.

Lili is poorly equipped to be a star because she sees too much and she doesn't enjoy being adored. And in that respect she lets them down because they want a real star.

I spent my first morning on the set trying to find out what "Dartey isn't really unattached" meant. It was difficult because Lili was rarely alone but during lunch break Lili explained that wherever she and Dartey went in the future his mother would always be an oppressive presence, either physical or mental, and she was not sure she wanted to take that on. She showed me some of the letters his mother had written to the *Daily Variety* and the *Hollywood Reporter*. They were quite funny really. His mother has the most amazing imagination but they have done some harm to Lili.

This week there is an article in the *National Inquirer* based on information from his mother and I've heard people whispering in the make-up van. They wonder if Lili is going to prove unreliable and stop production. The article says that she has brought two films to a halt because of her unco-operative behaviour and her drug habit.

Lili does not bother to explain to anybody that until quite recently her roles were so small they wouldn't even bring about an extended tea break. Lili just laughs about it all, although sometimes when she's tired it depresses her. Mostly she is depressed about Dartey. She thinks this behaviour of his mother reveals that he is tied to her. Lili seems to think that if he were free his mother would not behave like this.

I offered to write scurrilous letters about Mrs Dartey to all the papers accusing her of being a Nazi war criminal or a former madam but Lili said it would not help.

185

On the good side the news is that everyone is pleased with Lili's performance. When she first started they asked her to play Hilda with an American accent but it changed her performance, "the money performance" as they called it. Now she's back to being English, Hilda having become overnight a GI bride.

I have become friendly with a cynical sound man called Hugo Berent. Whenever anyone says that the film will be a hit and the dailies are just fine Hugo says, "I never saw grapes that wouldn't make wine and I never saw dailies that weren't just fine."

The location for the last four weeks has been an old clapboard house in an overgrown neglected area of the San Fernando Valley. The yard in front of the house is adorned with a rusty old pick-up truck with no wheels, the top half of an old trailer and several dogs and chickens. This, supposedly, is the Californian equivalent of a terrace house in Birmingham. Eleanor's furious as she regards this "tumble down shack" as a personal insult.

"Everyone knows the story's about my family. We were working class but we weren't tramps. My mother's kitchen was as clean as a whistle."

Watching the filming is painful for Eleanor. She drops me off and then decamps almost immediately. She goes off to a studio to pitch ideas. Yesterday she went to MGM and tomorrow it's Paramount. She's promised me that I can come with her one day and present myself as her co-writer. I'm trying to think up an idea. Everybody on the set has an idea. They're all writing scripts. I don't want to be left out.

The director of the film is Ted Kavan. He is a dark-haired plump youngish man, intense and quiet, who chews his nails when he's thinking. He's been to Harvard and UCLA film school and somewhere along the way lost any sense of reality except film reality. Film is his celestial kingdom, his Mount Olympus. Lili says that he only sees actors in terms of their harmonious integration into his film. Other than that they do not exist. Lili says that when she's with him it's only by an act of will that she remembers that she's not a piece of celluloid with perforations either side.

186

Ted is over schedule and over budget. The studio is complaining that he's covering his shots too much and there is a general air of panic. The only people who are relaxed are the extras: they are delighted to be working and pile their plates so high with the free lunch that I feel sure they take half of it home to feed their families.

There is something very erotic about a film set. Sexual interest vibrates the air and threatens everyone. I asked Hugo, my cynical sound man, why working on a film was such an aphrodisiac and he said it was all the waiting around with nothing on your mind. Whatever it is, every film has its score card of new romances, broken marriages and general infidelities. Lili is unaffected by it. I think it's because she's thinking about Dartey all the time even if it is in a more disenchanted rather than pining way.

Lili doesn't sit around and chat very much when she's not in front of the camera. She disappears into her trailer. Sometimes I join her but it's rather boring to be with Lili when she's preparing herself mentally, so most of the time I go and chat with Hugo.

Hugo started work at Warner Brothers in 1947 when he was eighteen. Since then he's worked at all the big studios and met most of the old stars like Humphrey Bogart, Clark Gable and Judy Garland. We have long discussions about the decline in the stature and magic of the movie star. Hugo thinks that as the age has become more materialistic, humanity has diminished, that in order to have great stars you have to have a great human race. He thinks that people are losing their way and it's reflected in the sort of stars they have, wishy washy he calls them.

The most fascinating thing about a film is its power. When a film crew reaches a location, they become the location, the centre of that particular universe. Residents of the area seem to accept the film as the new rule of order and the crew remain quite comfortable in the knowledge that they are the ruling power. A film is a completely time-absorbing, heady, exhausting addictive experience, and everyone involved in it is hypnotized into this new reality and forgets any other reality they may have had previously. Hugo says that this powerful mesmerizing factor is simply the almighty dollar. They're spending eleven million on this film which is just about average according to him but enough to have everyone dancing on a string.

This is my last piece of note paper. Eleanor says she will drive me to Save-on's on Laurel Canyon tomorrow so that I can stock up on more paper and pens.

Dear Parents,

Henry's beginning to look like his old self again. I think he was feeling low (partially at least) because you've been suffering so much over leaving Berkeley Road. I think when you get yourselves sorted out it will be a weight off his mind. He picks up on the atmosphere around him. Have you made up your mind about opening the tea shop?

Henry's having a marvellous time and everyone adores him. He comes to the set every morning and stays for the entire day as though he's employed by the film company. The crew tell him yarns and he writes everything down in his notebook. Then he stays up late every night typing it up.

The film's going well as far as I can see. Henry will tell you more about it than I ever could.

Must rush.

Love,
Lili

Dear Parents,

I'm having a great time here and have, contrary to your lack of faith, taken thousands of photographs. We will have slide shows ad nauseam.

This is just a quick note to warn you not to probe too much about Dartey if you talk to Lili. I think she's going to phone you at the weekend.

Dartey is a painful subject at the moment so don't ask too many questions.

I will talk to you at the weekend too and should be back on the 18th if they let me on the plane.

Love,
Henry

LOS ANGELES TIMES
CALENDAR

The first thing you notice about British actress Lili Smith is the profusion of pink gold hair. She says she likes brightly colored hair and changes the color of her hair "whenever I can afford it".

She can certainly afford it now. She has just finished starring in her first film *Help Me If You Can*. Earlier this year she played the same role on Broadway and now she has a large pile of scripts on her coffee table to select from.

She talked briefly about her early struggles which did not prepare her for success and leading roles. According to Lili Smith the most difficult challenge for any actor is a small role. "You come in with your one little line that tells you nothing about your character and background and you have to present a full-bodied person. Leading roles are easier in that you have more to work with."

A profusion of job offers seems to worry her. "Going from waiting to be chosen to making your own choices is lovely but . . . should I choose for myself, for my own advantage or should I choose with a thought for other people? How should I use this power? Does this power have something to do with being completely self-absorbed. If I think of others will I lose this power?"

Ms Smith has pale skin and a fragile appearance and throughout our conversation looked like someone trying to solve a complex mathematical problem. "I suppose this is a time in an actor's life when they go into analysis and do lots of charity work. I'm trying to find a reason for what I do. It's very hard. I mean, what use am I?"

Does the life of an actress require such profound analysis? "No. I suppose not. And that's very worrying too."

She went on to say, "Actors bring the same mental effort and passion to their work as is required to discover $E=mc^2$ or to find a cure for cancer, but are the results of equal value?"

She discussed Ionesco who said that art must have no meaning in order to be art and that this is what makes it important. She talked at great length but reached no particular conclusion.

Lili Smith seems a troubled actress, burdened with the necessity of finding meaning and value to her work. Were her anxieties a luxury that few actresses could afford? "Yes I think they are. But unless I can come up with an answer I don't think I can raise the necessary passion for acting."

Judging from the favorable reports from the studio there are a lot of people who hope she will come up with an answer soon.

Dear Lili,

Here I am back home. Journey uneventful. Fell in love with a flight attendant from Glasgow who swears she's coming to see me in Brighton. She has a brother who manufactures wheelchairs. Could be a good connection.

Things at home are all right except that the parents are incredibly bright and breezy all the time, as though they've taken a crash course in positive thinking. They're driving me crazy with their smiles and helpful vibrations. I think they've both swallowed a large happy pill. I can't wait for it to wear off. I'm used to seeing our mother slinking about like the wicked witch of the west.

Anyway, apart from that, everything is O.K. and I'm getting over the California to Sussex culture shock. I'm spending every spare minute on the book as I have so many notes now and I'm sending the opening chapters to a literary agent. It's time to shit or get off the pot.

Dartey phoned yesterday. He's just back from Africa and has been phoning you day and night for three days without any luck.

I told him you might have gone out to the desert to unwind. It was the first thing that came into my head.

I hope you speak to him soon Lili. If I were him I'd like to be put out of my misery as soon as possible.

Love,
Henry

The last person to see Lili was a maid at the Mark Hopkins Hotel in San Francisco. The maid remembered her as the young lady who never left her room. She was usually sitting on a chair by the window looking down the steep hill which led to the heart of the city. She sat there for about three days.

Lili had fled north from Los Angeles with a large collection of scripts under her arm with the intention of finding some momentary peace and quiet to study. But once in the calm and impersonal solitude of the hotel room the larger issues of her life presented themselves.

Peering out from the centre of the morass which most people called success, she saw only that the original shining vision which had propelled her along the road, always ahead, always shining, now seemed to have slipped behind her and was retreating with frightening speed.

She was not so spiritual, so elevated, that she did not enjoy the worldly attention that she now received. Her film had not yet appeared before the general public, but the word was going around that she was about to become a marketable property. While the people in the business waited to see if this was in fact to be the case, they all smiled at her. She loved the smiles but they also disturbed her. She did not know exactly what had produced them. She did not know how to keep them there. She was told that it had something to do with an X-factor or personal magnetism.

There was a complete lack of principle behind it. She had

always assumed that a theatrical career could be based on sound laws, that a piece of drama and all the people in it were drawn together in a pattern that was as regulated as a musical composition or a mathematical equation. She had seen acting as both an art and a science, its pinnacle being reached by putting aside self and purifying the vision.

Now it appeared that her future was dependent on some indefinable personal charm. The vision which had been infinite had been reduced to a minuscule and dull dimension. Ahead of her on the long road she could see a life of unavoidable self-involvement as she tried to reproduce this charm. She had thought that devotion to an artistic cause would result in some release or loss of self but all she could see was the onset of a crabbier and narrower self-interest if she were to follow the course open to her.

Success was curiously unsurprising and not nearly as wonderful as she had imagined. In fact success was like a unique variety of failure. She longed to do something that was neither failure nor success, that was simply worthwhile and not open to misinterpretation.

On her third morning in the hotel Lili was up before dawn. A freezing mist swirled in over the bay. The city was very still. An early riser taking a shower thundered his presence along the hotel pipes. It was the only sound in the otherwise spiritual stillness before daybreak.

As the light slowly appeared Lili became aware of Dartey's face appearing and dissolving in certain formations of the mist. She wanted to stretch out her hand and touch him. She wanted to talk to him. It was around midnight in London; she could phone him now. It gave the day a curiously unfinished feeling when she did not talk to Dartey. She wondered why she felt incomplete without Dartey when she had felt perfectly complete before she met him.

The mist gently lifted and Dartey's face disappeared. Lili was gripped by a new and frightening sense of isolation. She knew that she would not phone Dartey, that she would not see him again. The conviction had been growing and now it was a solid fact. She would not go back to Dartey.

She would not go back because of Catherine—not so much

because of Catherine's insane behaviour but because of Dartey's attitude towards her. It was hard to define and even harder to discuss and if she were to take Dartey's advice she would see its insignificance and ignore it. But she had been in turn noble, understanding and occasionally witty about it but now she was coming to the miserable realization that she could not live with it.

To live with Dartey would be to live with Catherine because the shadow of her was always with him. To some extent the shadow of any man's mother was always with him. But in Dartey's case it was a shadow of unrelenting jealousy and ill will that was, as far as Lili could see, encouraged by his vacillating attitude. Catherine would continue to try everything in her considerable book of tricks as long as she thought Dartey didn't mind.

Rather than be drawn into an unasked-for competition with his mother, Lili would withdraw.

When the maid came in later that morning she noticed that Lili had been crying. Her face was blotched and puffy and she seemed to have no strength in her arms as she collected her possessions together. But in spite of this, well before the maid had finished changing the sheets, Lili had packed and gone. She left behind a large collection of film scripts.

Dear Lili,

I have been in Los Angeles for the past week and have looked everywhere for you. I'm giving this letter to your maid because she said you will be back soon. At least I think that's what she said. My Spanish is very poor. I believe she said that you packed very few clothes, which must be the reason she thinks you will be back soon.

I'm staying at the Tropicana Motel on Santa Monica Boulevard near La Cienega. I'll be there another two weeks until April 10th and I'll keep on looking for you. So far I've sleuthed all over Hollywood and Beverly Hills and have been offered a job twice. I've been out to the desert—much too large. I've talked to most of the people you've worked with and no one has a clue. I've spoken to your agent who is going quietly berserk over missed costume fittings for your next film and the small matter of signing your contract.

Someone gave me a copy of your interview in the *Los Angeles Times*. I've worked through it a hundred times but can only detect a certain disenchantment. Otherwise it sounded like the normal overly analytical Lili, nothing which would presage a sudden disappearance.

If nothing else, just let me know you're all right. Please get in touch.

I love you.
Dartey

Dear Lili,

My two weeks are up. I've looked everywhere, tried everything. I'm going back to London.
I miss you terribly. I can't stop loving you.

Dartey

Dear Gabrielle,

London is cold and dreary and my back is hurting again. I've given up expecting that you will write a letter.

Edmund has gone off to Africa again. He's changed and I can only put it down to the influence of that girl.

I had a terrible attack of pleurisy just before he left and he didn't stay to keep an eye on me. I thought I was going to die and was in urgent need of help, but he said he couldn't stay and off he went.

He just doesn't seem like himself at all. That girl has him in her clutches and he can't think straight. I doubt if I'll ever see Edmund again.

But I'm coming to see you. I'll be in Baden Baden on May 2nd. So find me a nice hotel that's not too far away from you. Phone me when you've made all the arrangements.

Catherine

KASSALA, SUDAN   July 16th 1986

Memo to DAF headquarters in London

Nearly all DAF staff have left the Equatorial region in Southern Sudan now that rebel fighting has spread from Bahr El Ghazal and Upper Nile. Four of our Juba staff remain.

Road travel between Juba and Nuimule on the Ugandan border is now extremely dangerous. Yesterday the airport was closed down which cut off the airlift from Uganda. The situation is very bad. Emergency food stocks in Juba are down to fifty tonnes. Unknown numbers of refugees are starving in outlying areas.

All trucks have been grounded since nine Kenyan drivers were killed in an ambush. Heavily armed bandits, some remnants of the defeated Ugandan army and soldiers from the Sudan People's Liberation Army have rendered safe delivery of food almost impossible.

One of our trucks has been stolen by Edmund Dartey who continues to deliver grain to Juba on a regular basis despite the current emergency. This is the only truck in use at present as all our drivers say the conditions are too dangerous. Dartey has sent two repair bills to our office which amount to £145.32p.

Memo from Bert Hahn to DAF office in Kassala, Sudan.

What's Dartey trying to prove? Does he have a death wish? Make him pay his own bills and tell him to get his own truck.

Dear Mr Hahn,

As you may or may not remember I worked in the DAF mailing room last year for a few months. I am currently working on a biography of my sister the actress Lili Smith who disappeared in March this year. The book has received a great deal of interest from the publishing world since my sister's disappearance. I am hoping that its publication will help me find my sister.

Lili had a friendship with one of your former employees Edmund Dartey. I would like to include a photograph of Mr Dartey in the book as he figures quite largely in it. I have tried to contact Mr Dartey but apparently he is in Africa and has left no forwarding address.

If you would send me a photograph of Mr Dartey I would be very grateful, particularly if it were a photograph of him in a working situation.

I enclose a contribution to DAF.

Yours sincerely,
Henry Smith

Dear Henry Smith,

Enclosed are some photographs of Edmund Dartey taken in Mali and Chad in 1984. I hope you will find them useful for your book. Please send me a copy when it is published. I wish you good luck in the search for your sister.

I cannot offer you much useful information about Mr Dartey as he no longer works for us. DAF is a busy relief organization and we do not have time to supply biographical details of our former employees.

Yours truly,
Bert Hahn

Dartey lay on a bed in a shabby room at the Africa Hotel and smoked a cigarette. He was not a habitual smoker but lately he had smoked more than a few. He could see from the dim light provided by a flickering bulb that his fingers were now heavily stained with nicotine.

Below in the street government soldiers clattered by in a noisy vehicle and fired their guns into the air. The sound of the shots echoed for a while and then a calm descended. The sun went down and the dowdiness of Juba was veiled and thus ennobled by the night.

Dartey had no more cigarettes. He would have to go downstairs and rustle one up from somewhere. The atmosphere of unease and fear which encompassed Juba that night was a contributing factor to his need to smoke but only a small one. He felt removed from the fear. He simply needed the comfort and distraction of smoking.

Earlier in the evening he had cadged half a packet of Benson and Hedges from an American called Jerry Bittle. He was a magazine photographer who had flown down for a day and stayed for over a week. He was anxious to get back to the Khartoum Hilton as soon as possible.

"Although," he told Dartey, "I'm not safe there. I was chased all over the hotel by this divorcée from Cleveland." He held out his hands to indicate a great width or size of some part of the woman's anatomy. "She has a Ph.D. in something or other. And she was threatening to come down here to study the troposphere . . . I think it was the troposphere."

"We're all coming," said Dartey, "all the arse-holes of the world. We all want to be here."

"I don't want to be here. As soon as they open up that fucking airport I'll be out of here."

Sporadic gunfire from the direction of the airport indicated that there would not be an imminent escape for Jerry Bittle. And here in the Africa Hotel the fading flickers of the light bulb were signs that Dartey would soon be released from contemplating the squalid interior of the room.

He needed a shave. If his beard grew any more he would begin to look like one of those nineteenth-century explorers who came up the Nile and died of a fever. As it was, he had a sensation of slipping back in time trying to find something to hold on to. Perhaps he was destined to lose a century or more and end up across the river from Juba at Gondokoro, the old slave trading post, peering at hapless Dinka men and women who were going to be sent down the Nile in chains. Like those intrepid men he would not only have to cope with the heat, the smell, flies, rats and malarial air, but also the antipathy of the slave traders for people outside the business. A white visitor who stayed too long might accidentally be dispatched by a stray bullet.

It seemed to him that things had not changed. Wherever he went people were cowering in fear and he had spent the last few months avoiding stray bullets. Right now he was too tired to feel guilty about enjoying the danger, or rather being grateful for it, grateful for its all encompassing power to engage his thought. In any case here in the relative safety of this room there was no such engagement. A thought pattern, like a computer loop, which produced an unending series of useless messages, set in for the night. The nights were always hard.

It was now almost six months since he had seen Lili. His analysis of the situation never varied. Out of the pain would come curiosity, first a compassionate curiosity, followed by a more hard-headed look at Lili and the pressures she was under, then he would be annoyed by her selfishness and finally rest in a dull anger.

He had almost daily illusions of meeting Lili. She would appear on the passenger seat of his truck, she would slide into his bed, or would phone him from London or New York. Sometimes he slapped her so hard across the face that the sound cracked the ceiling; other times they would fall into one another's arms, providing him with erotic and uncomfortable phantasms that left him even more angry.

He knew that he would soon grow tired of being angry. He also knew that he would never see her again. He planned in a thousand ways how he would react if he saw her suddenly but he would not see her suddenly. She was holed up somewhere avoiding him, avoiding the world. There was nothing he could do about it.

There was nothing much he could do about anything.

Driving his truck back and forth in showy acts of derring-do was almost meaningless.

"What you're doing is too fucking dangerous," Jerry Bittle had said. "And for what? It's just a drop in the bucket."

Bittle didn't understand that he had no choice, that he needed to be among people with a tenuous grasp on life, then his own equally slippery grasp did not seem so pathetic.

The light bulb made one last desperate flicker and then went out. Exhaustion overcame the need for a cigarette and he fell asleep to the faint, almost seductive, sound of gunfire.

Dear Mr Hahn,

Many thanks for the photographs of Edmund Dartey. They will both be used in my book, *The Life and Times of Lili Smith*, which will be published early next year. I will give you a brief credit in the preface and of course send you a copy.

I am enclosing a leaflet on my new venture into the manufacture of lightweight colourful speedy wheelchairs called "Superollers". They can be made to order and come in a range of exciting colours and reasonable prices.

> Sincerely yours,
> Henry Smith

Early in the morning Dartey drove out of Juba along the Northern Rumbeck Road. He passed a group of Mundari tribespeople who were moving towards the Nile bridge where they would make their escape if the rebels came along. Several small children ran in front of his vehicle and he swerved gently around them which made them laugh and wave their hands.

The heavy DAF truck which he had purloined and loaded with grain in Nuimule was watched with obvious concern by the Mundari men and women as they saw supplies moving out of town. He had dropped off half his load in Juba and was taking the rest on to Wau, truly a drop in the bucket as Jerry Bittle had said.

The Northern Rumbeck Road was riddled with pot-holes and deep ruts but Dartey rattled over them at an uncomfortably fast pace. Whenever he sensed danger he sank low behind the steering wheel, put his foot down hard and charged forward so that the truck hurtled along like a crazed rhinoceros. So far, obviously, it had worked. He did not care too much if it didn't. One thing Dartey no longer felt was fear. He was aware of danger as a mental challenge. That was about it.

The road led over the flat marshlands of the Southern Clay Plains. The tall grasses along the route were high enough in some places to hide his truck or serve as a hide-out for men watching him.

But neither the Sudanese People's Liberation Army nor government troops nor even a bandit stopped Dartey. He was lucky. He seemed to be consistently lucky, in this respect at least. He passed many Dinka villages with their familiar conical roofs of straw and sticks which must have housed rebel soldiers but none blocked his path. He knew that the SPLA considered any transportation of grain as support for government soldiers and therefore a direct threat to them. And he knew that only the day before an old woman had been hacked to death by bandits as she tended her vegetable plot and whole villages had been burned to the ground.

Twice he was shot at and once a Land Rover pursued him for a short distance and then gave up for some inexplicable reason, mechanical trouble perhaps. Whatever it was he was in the clear and he stayed out of trouble for the rest of the day.

When night fell he drove the truck into the long grass and waited for a few hours. He did not sleep but sat listening to the eerie night sounds. At first light he moved on.

It was early afternoon when he drove in to a refugee camp south of Wau which housed about fifteen hundred frightened villagers. He was told that they had enough supplies there for a bare subsistence but even so, many were leaving because they were afraid to be outside the town. Those who went into Wau looking for safety were in greater danger of starvation however. The little food there was being hoarded and sold at prohibitively high prices. A kilogram of lentils was being sold for twenty pounds sterling. Families were huddled together on the street, too weak to move, staring into space. Remaining stocks in the town, three hundred and eighty tons of relief food plus one hundred tons of merchant food, to cover the needs of one hundred thousand people would possibly last two weeks if handled carefully, but if subject to greed and panic the town could be completely without food in five to six days.

Dartey was approached by a young Finnish student whom everyone called Jon and whom he had once met in Khartoum. They spent an hour drawing up elaborate and slightly utopian plans to bring an immediate convoy of supplies from Uganda guarded by several tanks and machine guns, which helped their frustration if nothing else.

Jon told Dartey that he was about to drive two of the camp workers into Wau to catch a plane to Khartoum as they had been given a week's rest. Flights out of Wau were hard to get and they were all booked up weeks in advance. Flights in to Wau gave passengers a taste of things to come when the pilots did a tight spiral into the airport to avoid being shot down.

Dartey walked slowly through the camp talking to people, listening to their stories. He went towards a tent where a relief worker, surrounded by a gathering of mothers and children, was bending over a large bowl of soapy water intent on washing something. As he drew near he saw that the relief worker had thin arms and rough hands like the women around her but, unlike them, she had eyes that looked set in a permanent squint under the harsh light and skin that had reacted badly to the sun. Her face he had seen a thousand times in the past few months. It was Lili.

Immediately he drew back. A gut reaction. There was not much he felt capable of doing beyond standing there and watching her, unnoticed. He wanted to avoid making it real and unpleasant by getting any nearer. They were complete strangers. He knew nothing about her. He could stand there and learn something about her from the way she related to the women around her and from the way she washed those objects which now seemed to be small orange plastic bowls. She worked quickly and efficiently like someone who was used to

201

her work and accepted it and those around her as a proper part of her life.

Dartey slowly became aware of the fact that he was half crouching behind a bush like a peeping Tom, transfixed, hypnotized by the performance of a simple everyday task.

Lili picked up the clean orange bowls, gave some to the women around her and took the rest into the tent; then she emerged and took the large washing bowl inside. She came out once more and started to walk towards Dartey. As she drew nearer, Dartey could see the resolute expression on her face but she could not see him. She went to a nearby bush and threw a piece of towelling or cloth over its branches. Then she went back to the tent.

It was the Finnish student, Jon, who ended the impasse. He drove up hurriedly in a Land Rover to collect Lili having left it rather late to take her to the airport. Already he had one anxious passenger and he was feeling guilty.

He saw Dartey crouching awkwardly behind a bush and called out to him. Dartey stood up and began backing away as though he had suddenly remembered a compelling engagement elsewhere. Lili came out of the tent with her plane ticket tucked in her belt.

Jon shouted to Lili that they would have to rush and she glanced at Dartey, turned and went straight back inside the tent. Dartey, he noticed, continued to back away. Meanwhile Jon was revving the engine as a sort of loud alarm call to Lili. When that didn't work he backed up to get nearer the tent.

Swearing quietly to himself Jon jumped out of the driving seat and went inside the tent. He found Lili crouching on the floor arranging and rearranging a pile of plastic bowls. Her face was blank, almost frozen and she seemed unaware of his presence.

"What the hell are you doing Lili! We should have left an hour ago."

She looked up at him, then went on arranging the bowls, first in four small piles, next in one large pile. She repeated this action over and over.

Jon wondered if he was witnessing some sort of breakdown. He felt ill-equipped to deal with it. He was only a student observer and if he had any skill at all it was in engineering. He stood there shifting from one foot to the other, looking at his watch and wondering if he should go without her.

At last, as if suddenly inspired, Lili put the bowls into one perfect pile, stood up and took her plane ticket out of her belt. She gave it to Jon with an air of total concentration which, he discovered, she needed to keep the ticket steady. When for one instant the concentration left her, her hand was convulsed with an uncontrollable shake that they both tried to ignore.

"I'm not going," she said. "Give it to someone else."

Jon did not stay to watch any further unbalanced behaviour but raced out to the Land Rover and drove off as fast as the milling refugees and the rutted track would allow him.

As he drove away he could see that Lili had emerged once more from the tent and was now framed in his driving mirror. She was running towards Dartey who had managed to create a distance of about thirty yards between himself and the tent.

Dartey stopped and waited. Jon could see him lower his head in a guarded, self-protective movement. When Lili reached him he listened to her for an instant then he began waving furiously towards Jon, signalling in no uncertain terms for him to come back.

Jon swore once again. As he slowed down he saw Lili grab Dartey's hand to prevent him waving. She made a violent pushing motion with her free hand, signalling for Jon to go on.

The inexplicable discord and indecision between the two was no incentive for him to go back to them. Jon swore for the last time and speeded up. If either of them waved to him again he would pretend not to notice.

But they did not wave. The two figures in the mirror paused to watch him go, standing quite still, perhaps considering what to do next. Before they could decide they were suddenly distracted by something outside the periphery of his driving mirror and they moved quickly out of sight.

When he swung round on to the road he could see them once again. Dartey was holding a small child in his arms. Jon could not see who had presented the child to him, nor at that distance what was wrong. But he could see that both Lili and Dartey were engrossed in examining the child's motionless body. An acacia tree bowed towards them mimicking the almost reverential movement of their heads towards one another.

The three figures framed in the mirror seemed adrift from time and space—man, woman, and child drawn together and becoming one blurred whole. As the distance grew they became smaller in the mirror and the clusters of refugees and the thick tall grasses and exuberant vegetation of Southern Sudan engulfed them until they disappeared.

Dear Lili,

I hope you receive this advance copy of the book. My last two letters were returned. I must say it's hard to track you down even though you are now supposedly "found".

The book will be on sale in the shops tomorrow and you, mysterious and still in Africa with Dartey, will just be a face on the cover.

If this is returned, I'll deliver it personally.

Love,
Henry